Terror in the Shadows
Volume 1
Volume 1
Written by Ron Ripley, David Longhorn,
Sara Clancy, and A. I. Nasser
Edited by Emma Salam

ISBN: 9781724240101
Copyright © 2018 by ScareStreet.com

Thank You and Bonus Novel!

We'd like to take a moment to thank you for your ongoing support. You make this all possible! To really show you our appreciation for purchasing this book, we're giving away one of our full-length horror novels. **We'd love to send you a full-length horror novel in 3 formats (MOBI, EPUB and PDF) absolutely free!** This will surely make chills run down your spine!

Download your full-length horror novel, get free short stories, and receive future discounts by visiting www.ScareStreet.com

See you in the shadows,
Team Scare Street

Table of Contents

Jackson Stables
By Ron Ripley

The temperature had plummeted beneath the combined assault of rain and the sunset. Neil's thin sweatshirt was soaked through, and each drop of rain felt like a needle as it struck his exposed skin.

He shuddered and pulled his baseball cap down lower, water dripping from the brim. He desperately wanted to hitch a ride with someone, but he hadn't seen a car since he had left Litchfield, New Hampshire. It was as though everyone had known the storm was coming and they had hunkered down to wait it out.

Neil didn't have that option. He had been on the move for a week, moving south in an effort to get out of New England before winter hit. His whole goal was to reach Washington, DC before autumn, and at first, he had thought that he had a good chance of doing that.

But a week in Valley Street Jail in Manchester, NH had destroyed that possibility. He had been forced to find a flophouse for a week, renting a foul little room in Nashua and sharing a bathroom with everyone else on the floor so he wouldn't miss his court date.

And all because you had to fight a guy at St. Anselm's College, Neil thought bitterly. He had been drunk, of course, and the younger man's derisive comment about the Yankees baseball cap Neil favored had been unacceptable.

Campus security had pulled him off the student, and Manchester police had taken care of the rest.

I shouldn't be leaving the state, Neil thought, trying to warm himself. *I'm just going to get picked up somewhere and sent back here for parole violation.*

He shook his head and refused to think about it anymore.

Too cold, he thought. *Too damn cold. Need a place to sleep. Get warm.*

For the first time since the storm had begun, Neil stopped and looked around. A hundred or so feet ahead he saw a small road that branched off to the left, and there was a sign hanging haphazardly from an old granite post. Neil squinted and was able to read the faded words.

Jackson Stables.

Between the words was the silhouette of a horse's head.

Neil walked forward, speeding up. When he reached the turnoff, he saw how the underbrush had grown up around either side of the road and begun to spread across it. A sure sign that no one had traveled along this road for quite some time.

Neil hesitated, then turned onto the road. The branches of the trees on either side of the road formed a tangled canopy above him, and the rainfall was noticeably weaker.

Maybe there's a house, he thought, shivering. *Just someplace to rest.*

The sound of his feet on the old pavement was muffled as the trees and undergrowth became thicker. A glance down showed the asphalt was broken and crumbling on the sides with great cracks running along the center and perpendicular to the trees. Neil paused, shifted his backpack to sit so it didn't rub his lower back raw through the wet sweatshirt, and then continued along the road.

He felt the road rise slowly beneath him as the darkness thickened. Above him, he heard the rain striking the leaves, and while his momentum slackened due to his poor night vision, Neil felt comfortable.

Even if there's no place at the end of this road, he thought, *I'll rest here. This isn't too bad.*

Satisfied with his decision, Neil hastened along the asphalt, slowing down only when he reached the crest of the small rise and the trees fell away, leaving a wide, open field in front of him. In the distance, he thought he saw a large structure, and a moment later lightning flickered and illuminated the landscape.

Neil blinked, the image emblazoned upon the inside of his eyelids for a moment as he began to count.

One-one thousand, two-one thousand, three-one thousand, and halfway through four, he was interrupted by a thunderous roar that ripped through the air.

There had been a house. A monstrous building at the end of the road, and even in the storm he had been able to see how far away the structure was.

Probably a quarter mile, he thought, adjusting the straps on his shoulders again. *Across open ground. In a lightning storm.*

Neil glanced back at the dark road he had traversed and decided to make a go of it.

The place is dark, he thought. *There's got be a way in, and that sure beats staying out here.*

With his decision made, he put his head down and forced his tired legs to jog. Within a minute, his lungs complained, too many years of smoking having done their work on his ability to breathe easily. But he kept the idea of warmth and safety foremost in his mind and did his best to ignore the pain in his chest and the rasping sound he made as he breathed.

Several minutes passed, and a few more lightning strikes cut through the sky, each one closer to him. He concentrated on the thunder, on counting the time between the noise and the light. By the time he reached the building, Neil was gasping for breath, and there had been less than two seconds separating the thunder from the lightning.

His first impression of the structure left him ecstatic. The second caused his hopes to crash.

He had stumbled upon an old farmhouse, a large, rambling creation that had seen better days. Evidence of a fire was clear, even in the near darkness. The faded white siding was streaked with black from each window, and where the roof should have been, Neil saw only exposed rafters, each one protruding into the sky like a skeletal finger.

Reluctant to give up the idea of sanctuary so easily, he stepped up to a broken window, then peeled aside and gagged.

The house was rank with the stench of death.

Something, or someone, had died inside, and the body still rotted within.

Maybe a shed? A garage? he thought. Then he straightened up and stepped further away, a small smile playing across his face. *Stables. They had horses.*

A desperate hope filled him as he hurried around the right side of the building.

Maybe the fire didn't spread to the stables, he thought.

And when he turned the corner, Neil almost shouted out with joy.

Across a muddy and weed-strewn yard stood a stone and wood stable, and the roof was intact.

Neil ran to the open door and stepped out of the rain for the first time in hours.

The stables smelled of old hay and oats, horse and leather, and it was warm and dry.

Neil took his lighter out of his pocket, lit it and held it aloft, the small flame casting a surprising amount of light.

A full dozen stalls, stretched out to either side, all of their doors closed and ancient tack hanging on hooks outside of each. Saddles, equally old, hung over each door, and at the far left was a small tack room.

Neil advanced on the tack room, not bothering to look in the old stalls. When he reached the room, he found the door open, the room bare of any sort of equipment other than a small kerosene lantern hanging from a hook. He took the lantern down and gave it a slight shake.

Liquid sloshed inside, and he let out a surprised laugh. Sitting down on the floor, he raised the chimney on the lantern, adjusted the wick, and lit it with his lighter. A moment later a bright, clean light filled the room, and he lowered the chimney back into place.

"And let there be light," he murmured to himself.

Turning around, Neil closed the door, saw it had a lock and secured it. He shivered and held the lantern aloft. For the first time, he noticed a small bench built into the far wall beneath a window covered with an old bit of fabric. Crawling forward, he saw the hinges on the bench's top, and when he pushed up on the lip of it, the bench opened. A few spiders scrambled away from the light and the sudden disturbance of their home, but they didn't bother him.

His attention was fixed on the thick horse blankets folded neatly at the bottom of the bench.

This is just too good, Neil thought. He set the lantern down and removed three blankets. They were made of wool, heavy, and with more holes than was good for them. But taken as a whole, they would keep him warm.

Neil quickly shrugged off his backpack and opened it, removing a plastic bag that contained his only other set of clothes, the traveling meal he had gotten from a shelter, and his only pack of cigarettes. He set them neatly on the floor, then stripped down, his teeth chattering and his entire body shaking as he hastily wrapped himself in the blankets and let the wool warm him up. A gentle heat was thrown from the kerosene lamp, and after a few minutes, his shaking subsided.

The thunder cracked overhead, and the walls of the stable shook, but Neil grinned.

He was inside.

Humming, he opened his food and quickly ate it. When he

finished, he spread his wet clothes out on the bench to dry, and curled up in the blankets, resting his head on his backpack. While the wool was rough against his bare skin, it wasn't enough to keep his exhaustion from dragging him down towards sleep.

He felt himself drifting away, hoping that the rain would be done when the morning arrived.

A soft neigh caused his eyes to pop open.

Neil lay perfectly still, listening.

The sound wasn't repeated.

Outside of the stables, he heard the wind as it increased. The thunder roared again, but it was farther away.

I'm tired, Neil thought, closing his eyes. *Sleep in a stable. Smell the horses. Think I hear the horses. Nothing more than that.*

He relaxed at the thought and yawned as he made himself comfortable on the floor. The light of the kerosene lantern was bright, but he hated to put out the flame. He enjoyed the small amount of warmth it provided, and there it reassured him that he had not, in fact, left civilization behind completely.

In the morning I'll get on the road again, he thought. *I should be able to catch a ride. At least into Nashua. Maybe even over the Massachusetts border.*

Another noise filled the silence, and Neil had no choice but to remain immobile.

Fear kept his body frozen in place.

As a child, Neil's grandparents had been horse people. They had owned a few mares, horses put out to pasture before Neil had been born. But those horses, and others that followed, were a part of his childhood. He knew how to rub the animals down and to make friends with them, to get them to do what he wanted without resorting to force.

And he knew that while the wind might sound like a neigh as it coursed through an old building, it would never sound like hooves dragged across the floor of a stall.

Neil knew there weren't any horses in the stable. There was a distinct difference between the smell of a recently used stable and that of one which had been defunct for years.

The stable he was in had been empty. Perhaps for twenty or thirty years.

Which was why the sound of hooves frightened him.

He managed to break free of the fear, reached a hand out and turned the wick down on the lantern. The light in the tack room dimmed accordingly, and Neil waited and listened.

There was a chance, however slim, that someone might use the stable to get their horse out of the rain. If that was the case, then Neil would have to wait them out. And while he didn't particularly care for such a scenario, it wouldn't be the first time.

Neil didn't move as he lay on the floor. Didn't so much as twitch a finger. His ears strained for any additional sounds that might be audible over the pulse of his blood.

Silence.

He breathed slowly, counting each inhalation until he reached fifty, and he still hadn't heard another scraping hoof or soft neigh.

I'm hearing things, he thought, closing his eyes. *I'm tired. I might even have a fever, which wouldn't surprise me, not with me being out in that storm for so long. Try to find a hospital tomorrow, if I'm still hearing stuff.*

It took him several minutes to relax, and when he finally did, it took even longer for his need to sleep to overcome his alert state.

Neil drifted off, content and warm in his small nest of rough comfort, and he dreamt of a soft bed and his mother. He had seen neither of them in over a decade, not since he had turned twenty-five.

The sound of feet on the floor outside of the tack room door yanked Neil out of his dreams. He listened, and a moment later he heard the sound again. His eyes fixated on the door and fear built itself slowly and steadily in his system.

The old porcelain doorknob turned first to the right, then back to the left. There was a strained groan as the wood pressed against the doorframe, but the old lock was secure, and the door didn't open. The doorknob returned to its place, the dull gleam of the kerosene's light shining in the pale white porcelain.

Then the entire door shook as someone tried to force it open.

Neil clamped his jaw together tightly, refusing to utter a single sound.

Go away, he thought desperately, *just go away. There's nothing here. Only me, and I'm not worth your trouble.*

The walls rattled with the force behind the unseen person's attempt to enter the room.

Neil pushed himself into a sitting position and reached for his dry clothes.

As soon as his hand touched his pants, the person on the other side stopped their efforts to get in. A heartbeat later, footsteps stomped away, and Neil heard an undeniably male voice muttering curses as he went.

Neil glanced at the window, saw that it was large enough for him to get out of, and decided it was time to get dressed. Even if the stranger didn't come back and try the door again, with a crowbar or some other tool, Neil would sleep better knowing that he was ready to escape.

He dressed quickly and quietly, and when he finished, he put his wet clothes into his backpack. The only article of clothing he didn't slip on was his boots. They were soaked through, and he hated the sensation of wet feet. His new socks were dry, and he wanted to keep them that way for as long as possible.

At least the door held, Neil thought, wrapping up in the blankets again. *It'll take a little more than rattling the doorknob and pushing to get in. Which is good to know.*

That slight reassurance helped him relax, but he knew it wouldn't be enough to enable him to fall back asleep. Not fully.

Cocooned in the horse blankets, Neil propped himself against the far wall with his backpack on the benchtop and his wet boots beside him. If the stranger returned and tried to gain access to the room, Neil could be up and out long before the door ever gave way.

A sense of satisfaction filled him, and Neil even dared to turn up the kerosene lantern. Beyond the thick walls of the stables, the thunderstorm continued to rage, the rain slamming into the glass of the window.

He allowed himself to relax, although as suspected he couldn't fall back asleep.

It's alright, he thought. *I've gotten by on less.*

His thoughts were interrupted by the sharp strike of hooves on the floor. Neil tilted his head and listened. The hoof beats were too many, some overlapping others, for a single horse to make in the confines of the stable.

Damn, is someone using this place to keep their stock? he wondered. It wouldn't surprise him. Land for horses was at a premium, and the stable was in excellent condition. A little maintenance would go a long way.

But as he listened, Neil realized he couldn't hear any of the stalls open. And even if the hinges were oiled on a regular basis, at least one or two of them should have made some noise.

The set of hooves stopped in front of the tack room, the horse on the other side of the wood snorted. A hoof scraped against the floor several times, and as Neil listened, curious as to why the horse was there, he learned the answer.

Something struck the door, the blow sounding like the crack of a cannon.

The wood split down the middle with chunks of the door

spinning out into the room while the entire door sagged in the frame.

For a moment, Neil was paralyzed, unable to move from the sheer shock of the blow.

But when the second one knocked the door off the hinges, he scrambled to his feet. Without bothering to grab his boots or his backpack, with his heart thundering in his chest, Neil threw open the window and scrambled out of it, and back into the storm.

He let out a low cry as he landed on his left shoulder, feeling the sharp and unmistakable sensation of his clavicle breaking. Trying not to regurgitate his meager meal, Neil panted as he got to his feet, the rain and mud seeping instantly through his thin socks. The rain lashed at his face while the wind howled through the ruins of the farmhouse. Lightning struck nearby and illuminated the yard. Neil's breath caught in his throat as he glanced around, his mind unable to accept the images his eyes gazed upon.

Five horses stood in the yard around him, their eyes fixed on him. They stood utterly still, and while his own exhalations crept out of his mouth and nose in white tendrils, nothing of the sort escaped from the horses.

Lightning flashed, and a moment later, a peel of thunder shook the earth. When it did, he struggled to accept the sight lightning had revealed.

He had been able to see through the horses as if they weren't there. And as if to reinforce the image, he had seen that all the horses were dry. Their manes were perfectly combed and elegant, their tails as well. Each hoof gleamed, and their eyes showed a disturbing level of intelligence.

The horses were dark colored, each a deep chestnut as if they had all been sired by the same stallion upon the same mare.

And they were tall, easily the tallest Neil had seen. He found himself wondering how difficult it had been to break them to the saddle.

The thought vanished as quickly as it had arrived, and he focused on the animals. He knew that the lightning strikes were playing tricks on his eyes. It was an impossibility, seeing through them. Whatever horse had been in the stable had been real enough to destroy the tack room door, and Neil had no doubt that the creatures could do the same to him, should they choose to.

He glanced at the broken window and the wrecked frame, and shards of glass served as a reminder to his body of the injuries it had sustained. His stomach rolled at the intensity of the pain from his broken bone, and among the cold rivulets of water from the rain, Neil felt the warmer flow of blood. The glass had cut him on the way through the window.

With his good arm, Neil wiped water off his face and wished for his hat and belongings.

Later, he told himself. *Come back for them later. Something's wrong here.*

He nodded at his own advice and took a cautious step toward the dirt driveway that led out of the yard.

The horses moved with him.

He tried a quicker step and the horses cantered towards him.

When he stopped, so did they.

Neil glanced over his shoulder at the ruined farmhouse and wondered if he could make it to the safety of the structure before the horses overtook him.

One of the horses pawed at the earth, and while the hoof seemed incapable of churning the soft mud and dead grass, Neil had no doubt as to what would come next.

His decision had been made for him.

He turned on his heel and sprinted for the farmhouse, a flash of lightning showing him a small back door at the building's center.

The horses let out a simultaneous, horrific scream, and charged after him.

Neil panicked as he reached the house, trying to pull open a door that needed to be pushed. Realizing his mistake, he gave the door a shove and tumbled in as it sprang open and slammed against the interior wall. The foul, putrid odor that had forced him into the stable to begin with, slammed into him, but Neil ignored it, plunging deeper into the darkness of the house. Behind him, the horses continued to scream, their voices raised in a disturbing mimicry of a human's.

He heard their hooves striking the walls, felt the house shake, and he let out a shriek of fear as he tripped over some unseen item in the darkness.

When he struck the floor, Neil threw up from the pain in his shoulder, feeling the ends of the broken clavicle grind against one another. He tried to get up, but his hands slipped in his own vomit, and he fell again. The horses continued their assault on the house, and rather than try a second time to stand up, Neil crawled forward.

Every movement was a symphony of pain, his head throbbing in time to the erratic beating of his heart. His body screamed for him to stop, and despite the adrenaline pumping through him, Neil felt the sharp bite of glass still embedded in him from his escape through the window.

Panting, he was dimly aware of the floor beneath him.

It was smooth in places, rough in others, as if some madman had taken a hand-plane and worked the floor over in various spots. There was no rhyme or reason to the pattern, and Neil found that particularly disturbing.

When the sounds of the horses faded to a dull roar in the background, Neil allowed himself to relax. He rolled over onto his back, sobbing at the pain in his shoulder while staring into the darkness above him.

There was a complete and utter lack of light in the house, even when the lightning flashed.

What the hell is going on? he asked himself, his breath hitching in his throat. *Am I dreaming?*

His body answered that question for him.

He was in far too much pain for it to be a dream.

Neil tried to calm down, but he barely succeeded in his effort to regulate his breathing.

Finally, after an indefinite period, he sat up. With his good hand, he reached out and tried to find the wall. When he did, he recoiled, for the wall had been damp to the touch.

No, Neil thought, extending his hand again and wincing at the sensation of the wall beneath his fingers. *It's sticky. Like it's weeping glue.*

He had a mental image of old wallpaper, the material hanging and peeling in long, ragged strips. Neil wiped his hand on his pants' leg and forced himself to think.

There has to be a way out of here, he thought. *And probably straight ahead. Most old houses are like that. A hall that runs front to back. That's probably what I'm in. The hallway.*

Following that line of thinking, Neil relaxed a little more. As he did so, he felt his muscles cramp up, and for the first time, he realized his feet hurt. Warily, he reached down and probed the wet sock of each foot and gasped as he discovered rough tacks piercing the fabric. Clenching his teeth, he pulled one tack out, and he squeezed his eyes against the pain until stars and checkered patterns reminiscent of an Escher painting played across the backs of his eyelids.

His breath came in shuddering gasps as he rolled the tack around in his hand. It was short and sharp, and roughly squared.

An upholstery tack, he thought. Trying to remember when he had last received a tetanus shot, Neil extracted the remaining tacks, counting nine altogether.

Okay, he thought, *behind me is the way out. Ahead of me is the way I came in and the horses are there too. There was a person with them before. Someone who tried to get into the tack room.*

Neil listened and realized the horses no longer made any noise. Neither did the house shake from their blows.

They're all back in the stable, he told himself. *They chased me away. More than likely, the guy who brought them is in the tack room, sorting through my stuff and realizing I didn't have anything. He'll put the horses in their stalls and take off. Probably some hick who drove his pickup down a backroad. I just need to wait until I hear the damn thing start up and leave. Then I'll be able to get out.*

Satisfied with his decision, Neil adjusted his injured arm as best he could and waited.

He had no way to judge the passage of time, but he heard the thunder fade away, then the rain slowed and came to a stop. From where he sat in the hallway, Neil listened to water drip down from the top floors. As his adrenaline rush faded, exhaustion swept over him, but he knew he couldn't fall asleep. Not again.

If he didn't hear the person leave, then he wasn't safe in the house.

Neil would have to try and make it out through the front, where the smell was the strongest.

Finally, unable to wait any longer, he managed to stand up. He forced himself to touch the repulsive wall and use it as a guide. Each step was an agony, pain shooting up through the soles of his feet, the broken clavicle a horror to suffer through. The wounds from the glass, which had formed thin scabs, reopened and bled freely. Neil felt himself growing dizzy and weak from the combination of fear and blood loss.

But as he traveled further into the house, the interior took on definition. Light seeped in from somewhere, and he was able to see that the walls were not wallpapered, but paneled. A mucus covered them as if some giant slug had spent the evening creeping over every inch of wood. Through the gloom, Neil spotted the front door and a long stairwell that led to the second floor. From a window through a doorway, he saw it was the moonlight that offered the small shred of illumination.

Neil paused and looked into the room, seeing the broken and abandoned furniture. It took him a moment to realize that the room's window was the same that he had approached when he had first found the house. Instantly his eyes peered through the gloom, seeking out the source of the stench, and stumbling backward when he found it.

The rotting corpse of a person lay sprawled across an antique fainting couch. In the soft light of the room Neil noticed that the body wore the same battered jeans and faded green sweatshirt that he had on.

And like himself, there were no shoes.

Only a pair of socks on the narrow feet.

Neil glanced down at his own feet, then back at the corpse. In the grim, sunken features of the body, he realized he was looking upon himself. The high cheekbones, black hair. And Neil knew that if he crossed the room and looked at the right forearm, he would see the faded tattoo of a panther he had gotten as a teen.

That's me, he realized, horrified. *I'm dead. I died here!*

Panic welled up within him.

Neil stood and stared, unable to tear his gaze away from the terrifying sight of his own rotting flesh in front of him.

"He went into the stable," a voice whispered, and Neil screamed.

Without looking for the speaker, Neil ran on his damaged feet. He didn't slow down for the door either, slamming into it with his good right shoulder and driving the door and its hinges through the rotted wood of the frame. Neil staggered into the front yard, tripped over the door and nearly fell.

But he managed to keep himself upright, twisting around to see the speaker.

A small man stood in the doorway. He was wizened and ancient. Thin gray strands of hair hung down in greasy clumps to his shoulders, his clothes nothing more than tattered rags that accentuated the thinness of his frame. His face was pinched, his eyes shining in the depths of his sockets. He tilted his head with the same interest as a crow might show a curious piece of roadkill.

"Listen," Neil said, his voice hoarse, "I'm sorry. I just want my stuff, and I'll take off, okay?"

"He went into the stable," the old man repeated.

"Sure. Whatever," Neil said, licking his lips nervously. "Like I said, I just want my stuff."

"He shouldn't have," the old man said.

"Yeah. I figured that out," Neil replied. "So, what do you say?"

"They don't like anyone in their stable." The old man turned around and disappeared into the house.

Before Neil could ask who, he had his answer.

A loud, brutal neigh filled the night air, and a heavy force slammed into the small of his back. Neil shrieked as he was thrown onto the wet grass. He was face down and awash in pain. His legs refused to respond to his desperate attempts to stand, and a slow, numbing sensation spread out through his arms. Frantic, he tried to dig his fingers into the soft earth, but he felt a hand on his shoulder.

Neil screamed when he was flipped onto his back, and again when he saw the old man standing over him. In the periphery of his vision, Neil saw the horses, all of them watching him and waiting.

"He went into the stable," the old man said, staring at Neil. "They didn't like it."

Neil wanted to respond, but the pain was too intense.

"You went into the stable," the stranger continued. "They didn't like that either."

The old man lifted up a small sledgehammer. "Try again."

"No," Neil whispered.

And the old man brought the tool crashing down.

* * *

Music Box
By A. I. Nasser

I hated the music box the minute I laid eyes upon it.

It was a Christmas present. Or at least I think it was. I never could remember what the occasion had been, but I remember feeling disappointed. I remember ripping through layer upon layer of awkwardly taped red wrapping paper, shaking the box that encased it, praying that it was the blue Power Ranger I had been nagging my parents about for months.

I also remember the smile on my grandfather's face as he watched me open the box, and the sudden silence that fell when I finally saw what was inside.

"It's handmade, Johnny!" my grandfather cried out, clapping his hands and rubbing them together, obviously a lot more excited about the present than I was. "It took me a while, but I got it done on time, yes I did!"

I couldn't stop staring at the small box. It was clear that my grandfather had gone through a great deal of trouble to get it done. With trembling fingers, I ran my hands across the smooth wood and traced the initials he had carved into it, JKA. Part of me wanted to break into tears, because even then, I knew that a music box was not one of the coolest things a twelve-year-old could get.

My father coughed, and I grudgingly looked up at him as he sat in his rocking chair, pipe in hand, dark eyes staring gravely at me. I could feel what he wanted to say just by looking at him. I could see it on his face; the constant lecture he gave me and my brother, Kevin, about how a man's character is defined by key moments in life.

And this is one of those moments, Johnny, his eyes said.

I looked at my grandfather and gave him a weak smile. "It's awesome!" I lied, holding it up for him to see and shaking it carefully.

My grandfather chuckled and slid off the couch, settling on his knees beside me. "You are going to love this, my boy," he said, taking the music box out of my hands. "You don't even have to wind it up!"

I watched him roll it around before finally flipping the lid open. A small wolf was at the center of a turning disc, carved in wood, howling at some non-existent moon. It began to turn, silently at first, before the music accompanied it.

"Dad, what is that?" I heard my mother ask from behind me.

I didn't need to ask her what she was talking about. I knew what was bothering her, what was driving nails into my skull and scratching at the inside of my eyes.

The music.

It was the music that turned my initial hatred towards the box into complete loathing. And it took every inch of willpower not to snatch my grandfather's present and toss into the fireplace where it belonged.

***

"I think it's cool," Kevin said that night.

We were lying in bed, the moonlight finding its way through the partially drawn curtains, shedding a silver glow on the floorboards between us. There was a light breeze outside that ruffled the big oak planted right beside our house, and the branches swayed and danced, giving us a mesmerizing shadow play. My brother and I often stayed up late watching the dancing shadows, giggling as quietly as possible so as not to wake my parents while we let our imaginations make up stories to the swaying images. It was a game we played often. But not tonight. Tonight we were content with just lying in bed, unable to sleep, too tired to do anything else.

"What is?" I asked.

I heard a ruffle of movement as my brother turned in his bed. "The music box," he said. "That wolf is really cool!"

I didn't answer. In my head, the wolf didn't matter. It was still a *music box*. Which meant that I was going to put it in the back of my toy box and forget all about it. Sure, there would be times when I'd take it out, find a special place for it on my bookshelf when my grandfather came to visit, just so he wouldn't be upset. But in my mind, I didn't want to have anything to do with it.

"Can you imagine what the kids at school would say?" Kevin chirped.

"I'm not going to take it to school," I replied.

"What?"

I almost laughed at the clear shock in my brother's voice, mixed with just a little bit of disappointment. A couple of months ago, he had caught a ladybug in a jar and had taken it to show-and-tell, earning him a gamut of mockery from the other kids in class. I wasn't surprised that the music box excited him.

"How could you not?" Kevin demanded, trying to keep his voice as hushed as possible in the midst of his outburst. "The guys would go crazy over that! Did you see the wolf?"

"Of course I saw the wolf," I replied. "It's not as cool as you think. Now go to sleep, already."

Springs squeaked as Kevin dropped back into bed, huffing in frustration, obviously angry at how his big brother wasn't taking the music box seriously. I usually found moments like this amusing, especially with that pout on his face that made him look like a duck. But tonight it was annoying.

"If you like it so much, you keep it," I said, turning onto my side and giving him my back.

"Really?" The bed squeaked again.

"Yes, really," I mocked. "Take it to school yourself. See how the kids make fun of you."

There was a long silence, during which I was certain Kevin was contemplating this new turn in events. I had just opened up an opportunity for him that he had probably not thought of before. He would ignore my warnings completely.

"No backsies?"

"No," I said. "Now go to sleep."

"Can I see it?"

I turned to look at him, sitting cross-legged in his bed, the shadow dance on the floor making it seem like we were in two separate boats divided by a silver river. The smile on his face was almost cute if I hadn't been annoyed by his insistence.

"In the morning," I said.

"But you said I can have it," Kevin argued. "So, it's mine now. You can't tell me when to see it."

"It's yours when I give it to you," I replied.

"Johnny, *please—*"

"Fine!" I hissed, turning around again and drawing the covers over my head. "But if dad comes in here yelling, I'm saying it was your fault."

I heard the springs squeak again and the familiar sound of Kevin's little feet scurrying across the hardwood floor. I closed my eyes, listening as he rummaged through my toy box for a few minutes before sitting down with a dull thump. Then there was only silence.

I turned around, frowning, lifting myself up just enough so that I could see him from over the edge of the bed. Kevin sat in the space between the closet and the foot of his bed, barely visible in the shadows, staring at the music box he held in his hands. I watched him quietly, waiting for him to open it, but he just sat there. It made me uneasy.

"Kevin?"

"It's beautiful," Kevin said softly, turning it around in his hands.

It wasn't what he said so much as how he said it that made me shudder, just a little. I felt the temperature in the room drop slightly, and my hands curled around the edges of my blanket, pulling the covers closer.

"Kevin, maybe we should just wait until tomorrow."

But he didn't listen. He set the music box down on the floor in front of him and flipped it open.

I don't know if it was the dancing shadows, or the way Kevin just stared at the damn thing, but the moment the music began to play, my body began to shiver uncontrollably. I wasn't imagining the cold anymore, either. It seeped under the covers and crept into my pajamas, sliding up and down my limbs like cold fingers leaving trails across my skin. The air grew heavier, too, and my breaths came in short gasps, as if something were pressing down on my chest and preventing me from breathing.

"Kevin?"

"It's so beautiful, isn't it, Johnny?" Kevin asked, finally looking up at me.

My heart jumped in my chest, and the cold fingers trailing across my body suddenly felt like claws that dug deep into my skin. Kevin stared at me with eyes that had turned a deep amber, and the smile on his face did not reflect the amused merriment of a nine-year-old who had just gotten a new toy. No. It was sinister, conniving, a smile that promised dark secrets that, if told, would drive a man insane.

"Isn't it, Johnny?" Kevin repeated, and this time his voice carried a harsh pitch that scratched painfully at the insides of my skull. The music coming from the box only made it worse.

"Close it, Kevin!" I said, cringing from the music's onslaught. My mind was screaming for mercy, demanding that I jump out of bed and run out of the room. Now. Quickly.

"Let's make music together, Johnny," Kevin hissed, his voice deeper now, foreign to my ears. He began to chuckle. "Let's make music. Let's make music. Let's make music!"

His screams rocked through the room so violently I was certain it would shatter the windows and shower me in glass. I screamed in return, feeling those cold hands latch onto my spine and twist, forcing me to arch my back violently under the entanglement of the sheets. The music coming from the box rose to a high crescendo that pierced my ears, making the pain in my head even more unbearable. My hands balled into fists and my nails dug into the palms of my hands.

And just when I thought I couldn't take anymore, when the agony coursing through my body threatened to rip me apart, the door to our bedroom flew open and my father stormed in.

"What the hell is going on here?"

His voice was a muffled bellowing in the midst of the ringing in my head. The cold hands that had held me withdrew immediately, and my body flopped down onto the bed. The music stopped and the pounding in my head slowly began to dissipate. The lights in the room came on, and my eyes fluttered open to see my father standing at the threshold of our bedroom door, enraged. His eyes darted between me and Kevin before finally resting on the music box.

"What are you two doing?" my father shouted, grabbing Kevin by the arm and hauling him to his feet. "Do you know what time it is?"

I tried to answer him, but my head reeled, and the world around me continued to spin out of control.

"This is ridiculous, you two!"

My vision blurred as I watched my father toss Kevin onto his bed. "We're going to have a long talk tomorrow, you and I. Now go to sleep!" He pointed an angry finger at him, then turned to me. "Both of you!"

I nodded weakly. My eyes darted to where Kevin grudgingly

crawled under the covers, his eyes watering with tears, rubbing his arm where my father had grabbed him.

"One more sound from this room, and there'll be hell to pay!"

My father looked at the both of us one more time before storming out, turning off the lights and slamming the door behind him. I waited for what seemed like an eternity before I turned to look at where Kevin was, his back to me, sobbing softly in the otherwise quiet room.

"Are you okay?" I asked.

Kevin didn't reply. I wanted to get out of bed and go to him, but the fear of my father suddenly walking back in kept me from moving. The pounding in my head was gone, and I briefly looked at the music box resting on the floor, discarded in the midst of the silver moonlight and dancing shadows.

"Kevin?"

"Leave me alone," Kevin whispered.

"Kevin, what happened?" I pushed.

"I said, leave me alone."

I sighed and turned around, drawing the covers up tighter around me.

It took an hour for me to finally fall asleep.

***

We forgot about the music box for a few months after that night. Well, not forgot, but decided to ignore it, as though that night had never happened. It was a family habit; maybe if we didn't speak about what bothered us, then it didn't happen.

Kevin avoided me for a couple of days; after that night and on the rare occasions when we had to be in the same room together, I could see how hurt he was that I hadn't said anything to our father that night. It was the ultimate betrayal. I was supposed to be the big brother, always there to have his back.

When he finally did forgive me, I was in the backyard fixing my bike. I saw him from the corner of my eyes, rolling his own bike towards me with its flat back tire. He waited for me to fix the chain into place on my own BMX, all the time shuffling his feet and looking away when I caught him staring.

"Didn't I show you how to fix that?" I asked.

"I still can't do it right," Kevin replied. "I tried, but it didn't work."

"So we're talking now?"

Kevin shuffled his feet and looked at me, then nodded.

"Here, let's take it to the garage."

I abandoned my bike in the driveway and led Kevin to the garage where we set his bike up on the small workstation my dad usually used for his 'projects'. I half expected my brother to just prop up on a stool and watch me like he usually did, but he was quick to help with the tools, and paid close attention to everything I did. It was clear he wanted to show he was not fooling around.

When I had finally patched up the hole, I lowered the bike and rolled it to one side where he could pump the tire up.

"Want to go to the comic store?" I asked. "Dad gave me my allowance. My treat."

Kevin smiled. "Maybe next time," he said. "I still haven't read the one I have."

I shrugged and pushed up onto the worktable, swinging my legs as I sat and watched him pump the tire.

"You know, I really am sorry." I said.

Kevin paused for a second, and without turning around, nodded.

"I didn't know what happened, Kevin," I continued. "It was so weird. Like I was dreaming or something, you know? You had these yellow eyes and—"

Kevin dropped the pump and covered his face in his hands. His shoulders rose and fell as he sobbed, and I quickly slid off the table and fell on my knees beside him. I wrapped an arm around his shoulders and pressed him to me. "Hey, what's wrong?"

Kevin hugged me, crying freely now. His body shook like a leaf in my arms, and I felt tears well up in my own eyes. I felt helpless.

"Kevin?"

"It scared me, Johnny," Kevin mumbled in my shoulder. "It was so dark and scary. I couldn't see anything. And I was cold."

I frowned, his words causing a chill to race through me. I looked over my shoulder at the door leading to the kitchen, contemplating whether or not to call for help, but quickly decided against it. Kevin needed me, only me, and calling either of my parents would be like breaking that trust again.

"Throw it away, Johnny, please throw it away."

I held my brother tighter, and my heartbeat raced when his shivering intensified. "Throw what away?"

Kevin sniffed, then let out a soft moan. "The music box," he said. "Throw away the music box."

*****

I looked for it with this very intention in mind; the only thought going through my head was that of getting rid of it once and for all. I was angry; enraged actually. I hated seeing my brother cry, and I searched for the music box with a vengeance. I had even taken my father's hammer from his toolkit, already picturing myself smashing the box to pieces.

It was at the back of my toy chest, cradled between a Thundercat and a smiling Mickey Mouse. I would have missed it if it hadn't been for the way the light had reflected off its polished surface. I pulled it out, tipping the toy chest over in my anger and almost tripping over the mess. I placed the box on my desk, raised the hammer, and then hesitated.

Key moments, Johnny, remember? How do you know that destroying it is going to stop whatever came after Kevin? What if you just unleash it into the world? What if Kevin's eyes turn yellow again and stay like that forever? Do you really want to do that to your brother?

I brought the hammer down, slowly, and rested it on the desk next to the box. I don't know how long I stood there, stoic, my eyes fixated on the music box. Ten minutes? An hour? I had no idea. All I knew was that my blind determination was probably going to cause more damage than good.

I shook my head, biting my lower lip as I reached for the music box, my hand wavering slightly above it before I snatched it up. I held it close, turning it over and over, trying to wrap my mind around what to do with it.

Bury it. Throw it in the river. Just don't, for heaven's sake, open it!

I opened it.

Several things happened at the same time the second that lid went up. The cold from that night came rushing out, as if from the box itself, and the hands that had once threatened to rip my spine in two latched onto my shoulders. Invisible claws dug into my skin, forcing my mouth open in a silent scream as a force pulled me forward. I clenched onto the box, but I couldn't feel it anymore. The disc began to spin, and as the music erupted, filling my head with its ominous tune, I could have sworn I saw the wolf turn its head towards me and smile.

Then there was nothing.

***

I opened my eyes to darkness, and a chill crawled into my skin, wrapping itself around every bone in my body. I sat up, the air around me a heavy blanket that strangled my every breath. I gasped. I choked. I coughed. And all the while, my body shook like a leaf in the wind. Somewhere in the distance I could hear water dripping, the sound of it echoing in the darkness, its source indiscernible.

I wasn't in my room anymore; I knew that for sure as I pushed myself up to a sitting position, my hands like ice against the cold stone floor. My ears were ringing, and I clenched my eyes closed, only then realizing that what I was hearing was the music box's tune. It was vibrating off the walls around me, soft and muffled, as if it were coming from somewhere on the other side of the wall.

Chains rattled, and I gasped, pushing myself against the stone wall behind me. My eyes searched the darkness but found nothing. I held my breath in an attempt to blend in with the darkness, but I couldn't hold it for long, and after a few seconds, gasped for air.

The chains rattled again.

"You opened the box, didn't you?"

The voice came from all around me, hoarse and heavy, the voice of an old man too tired to speak. It sounded familiar, but I couldn't quite place it. My head snapped right and left, and my heartbeat quickened. Still, I couldn't see anything.

"That was stupid."

The words felt like they were being whispered directly into my ear, and I scrambled away, blind to where I was going. A hand grabbed me by the shoulder, a vice-like grip that propelled me back against the wall as I screamed. My heart jumped into my throat and I kicked out aimlessly.

"Stop moving!" the voice hissed. "You'll only make it angrier!"

I felt tears sting my eyes as I rolled into a fetus position, pulling my knees as close to my chest as possible, trying to hide within myself. From around me, the tune from the music box grew louder, and the walls around me began to shake.

"I'm sorry, Johnny," the voice whispered. "I couldn't stop it. I tried, but I couldn't."

I froze, suddenly realizing who the voice belonged to. From somewhere far away, I heard screaming.

"You shouldn't have opened that music box," my grandfather said.

I looked up, and twin eyes of deep amber burned in the darkness directly above my head. Claws dug into my back, forcing me to scream, and I was suddenly jerked up and propelled into the air.

***

When I came to, I was lying on my bedroom floor. Someone was screaming, and the shrill sound of it pierced my ears and made me wince in pain. I tried to move, but all I could do was turn my head, the rest of my body numb and unresponsive.

My father stood at the bedroom door, eyes wide and mouth agape as he stared at me in what looked like a mix of fear and confusion. On the floor beside him sat my mother, screaming while she rocked back and forth, blood staining the front of her shirt. She was cradling something in her arms, but my vision began to blur the instant I tried to focus on it, and I couldn't make out what it was.

I blinked several times, and my head began to spin. I tried to speak but nothing came out, and I felt the world around me darken once more.

The last thing I registered before I blacked out was my mother screaming Kevin's name.

***

Entry 841, 20th of September 2017
Patient number 3206: Johnathan Keller
Supervising doctor: Dr. Henry Wilkins

Today's session with Johnny marks the last day for him at Lakevale, and it's a little ironic that I would have mixed feelings about this. As a doctor, a patient's positive progress and successful therapy should be celebrated, but I would be lying if I said I was happy to see him go. After eight years of seeing him every day, I can't imagine what life without our sessions together will be like. It's hard to not try to figure out what is going on behind those piercing blue eyes of his.

Nevertheless, the progress made has been one I am most proud of. During this past year alone he has shown a remarkable improvement in health, both mentally and physically. I've finally noticed some muscles on top of that lanky frame of his, and he's taken to actually combing his hair out of his eyes now. Some of the other doctors have even commented on how he has been helping other patients, as well as the nurses. He's come a long way from the quiet and lifeless boy that was brought through these doors eight years ago.

There is one concern I have about Johnny leaving the haven of Lakevale and joining the outside world. One which I believe should be properly addressed by the hospital before his release. The fact that his parents still refuse to answer our calls leaves the question open as to where he will go from here. It is obvious that, although Johnny has come to terms with killing his brother, his parents have not. I worry that the lack of a warm home will result in a relapse, not uncommon for patients like him.

Nevertheless, I have high hopes for Johnny. It has been two years since he's mentioned the monster from the music box, or said anything about the coincidental death of his grandfather on the same day Kevin Keller died. He has even stopped drawing those hideous yellow eyes that plagued his artwork for years. I truly believe that Johnny will continue to show this kind of positive progress in the years to come.

One thing I will not miss, though, is his sense of humor. Although it's a little too dark for my taste, some of the nurses assure me that it's going to help him fit in with today's society, and I can only hope that is true.

Speaking of which, he left me a goodbye present today, something he made himself. I felt a little uneasy when I first saw it, but it did confirm that he has finally gotten over his fears. Besides, the craftsmanship is quite impressive.

It's a music box. With a little wolf on a disc.

* * *

Lost Dog
By David Longhorn

Jogging.

It felt like a punishment for some heinous crime, not an enjoyable way to lose weight and get fitter. By the time Mark had made it to the beach, just half a mile from his bungalow, he was sweating freely. His feet were hurting, his lungs were burning, and he felt the beginnings of a stitch in his side. Gulls wheeled overhead, on the watch for prey or discarded junk food. Their screeches seemed to mock Mark's pretensions to athleticism.

Overdoing it, he thought. *First run of the year, after a winter of rich food and too much booze. Need to pace myself.*

He stopped just short of the steps that led from the promenade down onto the beach. Catching his breath, he looked out at the vista of sand, shingle, and a few rocks draped in seaweed. Taking deep lungfuls of air, he tasted the tang of the seaside. He had timed his run to coincide with low tide, so that he could pound along smooth, damp sand. He had forgotten that the stink from the various rock pools would also be present.

That seaside smell. Victorians called it ozone. Didn't someone say it was just rotting seaweed, really?

The thought of rotting organic matter conjured up unpleasant images, of drowned mariners and decayed bodies washed up on the tide. The storms of the winter had been frequent and intense. Harbor defenses had been damaged, boats wrecked, a few reckless people swept away. Vast amounts of debris of all kinds had littered the beach for weeks. Mark shook his head, took some more deep breaths, then started to jog again. The tide had done its work and left most of the sand pristine. There were no major obstacles. He was determined to manage a basic two miles this morning, and that meant pounding up the beach to the cliffs just below the old lighthouse, then back.

Easy peasy. I can do it.

After another hundred yards, he was not so sure, though. Again, he found himself gasping and sweating. Moving onto the soft sand from the concrete of the promenade had not made his feet feel any better. And the stitch in his side was still threatening to spoil his unambitious fitness program.

Mark slowed down, casting a glance around to see if any other early risers could see just how fat, red, and stupid he must look. There was nobody around. It was not long after dawn on an April morning that threatened rain. Perhaps all the other would-be joggers had looked out the window, turned over in bed, and decided to get an extra hour's shuteye.

Sensible chaps, he thought.

But then he saw evidence that he was not alone. A brownish shape appeared, far ahead, midway between Lighthouse Point and Mark. It soon resolved itself into a dog trotting along, just above the tideline.

Where there's a dog there's a dog walker.

Mark scanned the beach ahead for signs of the animal's owner, but could make out nothing even vaguely human in shape. The dog, meanwhile, continued to head towards him. When it was about twenty feet away, it stopped. Mark continued to jog gently forward, then slowed to a walk. He liked animals, appreciated their individual characters, their capacity for trust and affection.

"Here boy!" he said coaxingly, stopping so as not to spook the dog. "Here boy!"

The animal stood looking at Mark, its head cocked to one side. Mark made encouraging noises, then hunkered down, reducing his size. He knew that was a good way to make animals less nervous. But this one was not inclined to trust him, it seemed. And still no owner appeared on the beach beyond.

Odd. Maybe it's a stray?

As Mark studied the dog more closely, the notion that it might not have an owner nearby grew more plausible. It did not look quite right, somehow. He could not tell what breed it was, so he presumed it was a mongrel. Average sized, with a black and tan coat, the dog had an overlong, ragged-looking tail and rather stumpy legs. Its head, too, seemed oddly proportioned. It was lopsided, in fact, with one eye shoved an inch or two down and to one side by a bulge on the animal's skull.

Oh God, the poor thing.

The dog was deformed, perhaps as the result of abuse or disease. Mark felt a surge of pity, followed by anger. He was always outraged by the cruelty his fellow men could inflict on helpless beasts. Mistreatment of dogs, in particular, offended him. He spent too much time traveling for work to keep a dog of his own, and this only added to his righteous indignation when others abused canine companions.

"What's happened, boy?" he said. "No wonder you're nervous."

The dog seemed to hesitate, took a step towards Mark, then another. He reached out a coaxing hand, inviting the dog to lick his fingers and establish contact. But the animal seemed to take fright, its wonky eyes rolling in panic as it leapt skittishly away.

"It's all right, I'm not going to hurt you!"

But the dog was already heading back the way it had come. Mark noticed then that it had no collar, but that there was some kind of leash trailing from its neck, just long enough to leave a narrow groove in the sand. A greenish-brown cord? No, more likely a piece of string that had become damp and stained with seaweed. Mark envisioned a homeless person, perhaps a violent alcoholic, dragging the hapless beast around as a prop for use in begging.

Not fair, he chided himself. *Plenty of prosperous homeowners are complete bastards when it comes to pets.*

Mark stood, unsure what course of action to take. The dog, which had glanced back several times, stopped and turned to face him. Then it began to move in a wide arc, heading up the beach, keeping about thirty feet away from Mark.

Torn between two impulses, he thought. *A desire for human contact, friendship, and fear that I'll prove to be as brutal as its owner.*

The dog reversed direction, heading back to the tide line. As it did so, it gave an odd bark that sounded somewhere between a gasp and a laugh. The animal's expression, now as Mark thought about it, was quite funny. Its deformity, however tragic, gave it the look of a comedian expressing mock surprise. Smiling, Mark found himself thinking of an old nursery rhyme:

The little dog laughed to see such fun,
And the dish ran away with the spoon.

"Well, you do what you like, mate," he said. "I've got to get on. Need to get home, take a shower, and eat breakfast."

Mark resumed his run towards the point, again jogging at a very gentle pace. The dog continued to zig-zag ahead of him, keeping a stone's throw away, looking back as if to make sure Mark was following. After a couple of minutes, Mark could make out the jumble of rocks at the base of the cliffs, and the gaping mouths of the sea-caves beyond. The caves, he recalled, were only accessible for half an hour or so at low tide.

Somehow, the thought of getting any closer to those dark apertures made him uneasy. The nursery rhyme had churned up a host of other childhood memories, including fears of half-open cupboards, and the dread of monsters that his younger-self felt sure must lurk under the bed. The stitch began to assert itself again and he began to slow down, thinking to cut his run short and to hell with his fitness program.

"Sorry, doggie, I'll have to bid you farewell," he said. "Hope it works out for you. Hope you get home, or find a new one that's nice."

Mark stopped, bent to clutch his knees and catch his breath. When he looked up again he was startled to see that the dog had approached much closer than before. It was perhaps ten feet away now, and giving that odd half-laughing bark. At the same time, it kept moving back and forth, as if urging Mark to follow it. He assumed that it wanted to play. That was reassuring, suggesting the beast was not hurt, but Mark simply did not have the time now.

"I can't play with you, doggie!" he said, hoping his tone of voice would convey his meaning. "Gotta go home! Maybe tomorrow?"

The dog continued its back-and-forth movement, with greater urgency now. Something about the animal's behavior triggered another memory. One of many old movies he had watched.

"What is it, Lassie?" he asked humorously. "Young Johnny trapped down the old mine shaft?"

The dog tilted its head to one side as if trying to make sense of Mark's words. He felt oddly ashamed at having mocked the animal. It was as if he had poked fun at a disabled person. Again, he noticed the trailing cord, and this time he was close enough to see that the end was frayed, as if torn.

Someone's had an accident, he thought.

The realization brought panic. In a flash, Mark visualized any number of possible scenarios. Someone, very probably a venturesome child, had gone exploring the sea caves with his dog and got into trouble. A boy could be lying with a broken leg, or back, right now while he was making stupid jokes. Mark looked around to see if anyone had appeared, but all he could see was a faint red blob at the far end of the promenade. The blob was just perceptibly moving this way.

Whoever it was, it would take Mark at least ten minutes to reach them with no guarantee they could help. He felt the frustration, the near panic, of a twenty-first century individual cut off from his hyper-connected society at precisely the wrong moment.

Just then, a car sped into view along the promenade road, and was gone before Mark could even begin waving at it. Anyway, a driver would unlikely be looking down at a sharp angle to where man and dog were standing.

"Bollocks!" he exclaimed, feeling for his phone then remembering that he had left it on the kitchen table. *My not wanting to be pestered with work emails could cost some kid his life!*

"Okay, show me where they are!" he said to the dog and started to run again, heading up the beach towards Lighthouse Point. The animal kept ahead of him, glancing back at intervals to check on Mark's progress, its tongue lolling. Despite the sense of urgency, Mark had to smile again at the creature's comical appearance.

Sure enough, the dog led him over the slippery rocks towards the mouth of the nearest, and largest, cave. Mark slowed to a careful walk, then clambered onto the rock. The dog seemed to have fewer problems with the weed-slick surfaces that Mark would have expected, easily bounding ahead, and then stopping to let Mark catch up. A couple of times the man nearly fell, once catching himself with one hand and wrenching his wrist.

"Better not be leading me on a wild goose chase," he warned. The dog gave its laughing-gasping bark again, turned, and entered the cave. The rocks grew larger, more treacherous as Mark followed, and he realized that inside it would be almost pitch dark. He hesitated, and heard the dog's odd bark echoing against the stone walls urging him on.

"All very well for you," he muttered. "Four legs good, two legs not so good."

The cave mouth was much higher than Mark had thought, reaching up about ten feet above his head. He could see virtually nothing inside except an expanse of damp gray walls and roof.

What if the kid is in way deep? Maybe I should go and get professional help. Call the Coastguard, or the lifeboat service. Or just the police, they'll know what to do.

The dog's gasping bark was almost continuous now, as if the beast could sense his hesitation and was growing desperate. Mark looked around again, hoping against hope that another early riser would be nearby. Instead, he saw something peculiar that he had missed during his pursuit of the dog.

There were faint footprints in the sand leading towards where Mark now stood. They went one way. There was no sign that the person making them had returned along the beach. Here was positive proof that someone must have gone into the cave.

So why don't I feel reassured?

Mark gingerly took a few steps back over the rocks to get a closer look at the prints. They were clearly visible from a few feet above the beach, but so faint that it was not surprising he had missed them when running along the same route. *They are*, he thought, *the prints of running shoes, and quite small.*

A child's, then. Or a woman's.

The dog's barking was louder, and he glanced over his shoulder to see that the nondescript animal had appeared at the cave mouth.

"Okay, I get it," he said soothingly. "Somebody brought you out for your morning walk and they made a big mistake."

Mark turned to pick his way over the rocks. Again, the dog vanished into the dark interior of the cave. Mark took a deep breath and started forward, crouching despite the abundant headroom. Something about the situation seemed to require that he make himself small, try to go unnoticed. He wondered why the screeching of gulls seemed so much quieter, now. They were all far off, none circling in the updraft from the cliffs. As if they had good reason to steer clear. Wild creatures would sense danger long before the modern, urban man.

That's stupid, he told himself, straightening up. *Get a grip, you wimp! You're a grown man.*

Despite this, the old childhood memories continued to churn and roil. The wardrobe door that was never quite shut. The terror he felt at putting that first foot down on the floor when he needed to pee in the small hours. The staircase in his grandparent's house that had been so dark and steep, and impossible to simply walk down on. He had always run, dreading the imminent touch of the nameless thing he felt sure was stalking, or hovering, or floating just behind him.

For Christ's sake, focus! Stay in the here and now!

But in the present, too, there was unease. Something about the footprints niggled at the back of Mark's mind. His own, clearer prints had run alongside and sometimes over them. That was natural enough. But there was something else.

What is it?

So preoccupied was Mark with the stranger's footprints that he almost lost his own footing. Again, he caught himself, slamming his already injured hand against the cave wall. Cursing, he pulled his hand away, examined it. The flesh was not just abraded but slick with some foul-smelling gunk. He tried not to imagine what might have been carried in on the last tide, imperfectly suppressed murky visions of rotting organic matter.

"Where are you, boy?" he hissed, hoping that the dog would somehow lift his spirits, make everything right with the morning again.

The gasping bark sounded again somewhere ahead, but the echo made it difficult to be sure how far away the animal was. What's more, now that his eyes were adjusting to the cave's interior, Mark could see that the cavern divided about thirty feet in. The main cave continued to the left, curving away slightly. To the right, was a small cave or tunnel. It was only about five feet high.

Nobody in his or her right mind would go in there, surely?

"Where did you go, boy?" he said, raising his voice.

The bark certainly seemed to come from the smaller side-cave.

"Oh, shit!"

Mark picked his way gingerly to the entrance of the smaller aperture. It seemed to slope away down into utter pitch-blackness.

"Anyone in there?" he shouted.

There was neither a reply, nor an echo. It was as if something was damping down vibration.

Seaweed, he thought. *Great piles of it, probably, brought in by the tide. Whoever got into trouble probably slipped on it. Got a bash on the head for their carelessness.*

Mark crouched and shuffled into the side-cave entrance. Almost at once, a stench of rot struck him like a blow. There must have been tons of rotting seaweed wedged inside, perhaps accumulated over years. He could see nothing ahead but darkness.

Then Mark heard a noise.

It was not the dog. Something much bigger.

At first, he thought a person might be struggling to emerge. Yet there was something weirdly glutinous about the noise. The fetid air in the small space blew past Mark, ruffling his hair.

Whatever was moving was far bigger than a man.

Mark recoiled, forgetting his cramped surroundings, and banged his head on the cavern roof. Swearing, he fell over onto his ass, then shuffled out into the main cave, heaving a sigh of relief as he emerged into the feeble gray light. At the same time, as if jolted free by the shock, he realized what had been wrong with the strange footprints on the sand.

They had prefigured his own almost exactly. Whoever had made them must have approached Lighthouse Point, hesitated, made as if to go back, then reluctantly started to clamber over weed-slick rocks towards the sea-caves.

Just a coincidence.

Mark could not convince himself of that. And again, he heard the slopping, heaving sound from the side-cave, louder now and more urgent. Closer. He stood and started to back off, not daring to tear his gaze from the black tunnel mouth, feeling behind him for the main cave wall. The dog emerged, head on one side, tail wagging. But even in the poor light, Mark could see that it was no longer merely deformed, but almost melted-looking. It gave a fake bark that was now almost a belch, a canine impression so bad it was insulting Mark's intelligence.

What had been a good approximation of a dog's coat was flowing like hot wax, changing to greenish-brown and glistening tissue. The head was merging with the body, the eyes changing from warm brown to beady black. Stumpy legs became tentacles, as did the tail, and the floppy ears. The only thing that stayed almost the same was the trailing cord that had suggested a leash. It was longer, though, and trailed back into the side-cave. In the darkness of that rock tunnel something was moving, a pale shape emerging slowly, painfully, into the hesitant light.

What is it? What are they?

Mark's brain whirled and misfired, as it tried to make some sense of the trap into which he had walked. The dog-creature that had lured him in—was it a sub-unit, an ally, perhaps a symbiotic partner? Mark thought of deep-sea creatures in which the male was a tiny adjunct to the far larger female.

Does it matter? The bigger one might be slow, probably can't stand daylight! Just run!

Mark turned to flee, but out the corner of one eye, he saw a long, pale shape lash out from the side-cave. A stinging blow struck him on his already injured head and sent him reeling forward against the rock wall. The tentacle wrapped itself around his leg, a second grappled his arms, pinned them to his sides. A third coiled about his throat and started to throttle him. More sinuous limbs wrapped him in a muscular embrace and dragged him over the rough rock floor. He felt bones snap, his vision beginning to fade.

Mark began to scrabble at the sand that lay between the rocks of the cave floor. Suddenly he felt a sharp pain, one so intense that it cut through his fear. A familiar shape, curved and smooth, then jagged, dangerous. A broken bottle. He grasped frantically at the improvised weapon. But his arms were pinned. A phrase drifted through his fading consciousness, coming from God knew where.

Playing possum.

Mark let himself go limp. At first, it had no effect. The tentacles continued to wrap him painfully tight, dragging him across the weed-slimed granite. But then he felt a slight relaxation. He gulped air desperately, gave a great heave, and freed his arm. At the same time, he twisted his head round to see what had got him.

It was a writhing rosette of tentacles surrounding a circular maw lined with inward-pointing teeth. Fringing the fleshy cave of the monster was a ring of beady eyes. Mark cried in despair. The thing was too big to fight with the neck of a beer bottle. And he was going to be inside that serrated mouth in a matter of seconds.

A familiar gasping laugh came from just behind him. He recalled the living bond between the monster and its decoy, twisted round and slashed with the shard of brown glass. It was a lucky hit. The smaller creature, now reverted to its hideous, true form, jerked and leapt away. A jet of inky fluid shot out from the wounded predator, spraying Mark in the face. Stinging pain forced his eyes closed. But the attack had the desired effect. The tentacles holding him lost their grip as the pain of the lesser beast confused the greater.

Mark staggered upright and blundered into the cave wall. He

felt blood pouring from his injured hand, tried to wipe the foul fluid from his face with the other. He could just about make out the light of the cave mouth. Behind him he heard a glutinous heaving, felt a tentacle lash his left calf.

Don't fall down, don't fall down, don't fall down!

The mantra of survival ran through his head as he tripped, recovered, found himself among the rocks at the cave entrance. Adrenaline could only do so much and now the pain of the corrosive ink added to that from Mark's cut hand and broken ribs.

Blood loss will kill me, or at least make me faint, then that thing would reach out—

The familiar fake bark sounded close behind. He did not need to look to know that the decoy was after him. The Mark who had gone jogging at dawn could probably have kicked the thing to pieces. But he was wounded prey now.

He felt his ankle gripped by sharp teeth, glanced down to see that the creature had almost resumed its dog-form. He tried to kick it loose, and gasped in pain as the sharp teeth tore his Achilles tendon. He reached down and jabbed the creature in the face with his shard of brown glass. The lesser monster let go of him, and its false coat rippled, whitening in what must have been rage or fear. Black blood, not defensive ink, squirted from the lopsided face.

"What are you doing to that dog?"

Mark was so shocked to hear another human that for a moment he just stared blankly at the blurred form. A woman, to judge from her loud and disapproving voice, was just visible on the beach.

"I will report this to the police!"

Mark realized how bizarre he must look, and how culpable,

A blood-soaked maniac with a broken bottle fighting a mongrel.

"Help me!" he shouted, agony shooting through his damaged ribs. "It's not what you think—"

"You monster!" shouted the woman. "Don't think you'll get away with this."

Mark saw her raise her hand, and heard a distant click and whirr.

Oh, Jesus, she's taking a picture on her phone!

He began to clamber towards the onlooker over the rocks. She started moving away, gathering speed, perhaps running. His eyes were still streaming from the corrosive fluid.

"Keep your distance you degenerate!" she called. "I'll have the law on you, see if I don't!"

Suddenly, Mark realized that she was his best hope.

"Yeah, piss off you old bitch!" he yelled, hoping she would be outraged and call the police there and then. "You old cow!" he added, for good measure.

Again, the dog-creature fastened its vicious little teeth into Mark's flesh. This time it easily dodged his flailing attack, then jumped at his hand and fastened its jaws on his wrist. Screaming in pain, he dropped the bottle-shard, sank to his knees, and pummeled the creature with his free hand. Having disarmed him, it retreated again, giving its gasping laugh.

Nothing like a bark, really. Should have spotted that. Too easily fooled.

Mark tried to raise himself upright but seemed to be frozen on all fours. He was perhaps fifteen feet from the cave mouth, hidden from anyone on the cliffs above by the overhang. He felt himself growing cold, remembered that severe blood loss produced that sensation.

Well, at least if I die out here, that big bastard won't get me.

The thought was oddly reassuring. Then he felt small teeth piercing his wounded ankle again. The tugging that followed was shocking in its intensity. The small creature was vastly stronger than any real dog of its size. But it did have one thing in common with regular canines.

It's a retriever.

He began to kick out and scrabble at the rocks, trying to secure a handhold. Ropes of seaweed slipped through his fingers. After what seemed like hours, they reached the cave entrance, and the greater beast had secured him. The last thing Mark saw was a creature that was nothing like a dog, something like a walking squid.

But it still seemed to be laughing to see such fun.

***

"I tell you it happened right here!" insisted Marjorie Allington, gesturing at the rocks under Lighthouse point. "That awful man was attacking a poor little doggie! With a broken bottle, it looked like!"

The young police officer looked skeptical.

"Well, there's no sign of either man or dog now," he pointed out. "Obviously, if you wish, you can come to the station. We can fill out the relevant forms."

"Oh, really!" said Mrs. Allington. "Is that all you people think about? A helpless animal was being assaulted, quite possibly killed! You could at least search for some evidence. I provided you with facts!"

She held up her phone, showing a poor-quality picture.

"That might be a man tormenting a dog," conceded the officer. "Or he might simply have been playing with it, and you misinterpreted the situation."

The policeman looked doubtfully at the rocks while the woman spluttered with rage.

"I don't see how slipping on the weed and breaking my pelvic girdle would help the cause of animal welfare, madam," he said firmly. "Now, if you don't want to make a formal report—"

"Shush!" hissed the woman suddenly, laying a meaty hand on

the officer's arm. He was about to protest when she pointed towards the sea caves.

"Did you hear that?" she whispered. "I'm sure it was someone calling for help."

The officer frowned. He had heard something, perhaps a human voice, but the roar of the incoming tide made it impossible to be sure.

"Could be a seagull," he opined. "They can sound remarkably—"

The officer stopped in mid-sentence as a figure appeared at the mouth of the cave, crawling on hands and knees. It was diminutive, hard to make out at this distance. But it seemed to be a child wearing some drab green and brown garments. The figure raised a hand to wave slowly, in apparent pain.

"Help!"

This time, the cry was more distinct. It had a pathetic, gasping quality that stung both the onlookers to urgency.

"Okay," said the policeman, "you stay here, I'll check this out!"

Mrs. Allington stood watching as the young man picked his way over the rocks, all the while calling out in an attempt to reassure the little boy. Or girl. It was difficult to tell. The pale, almost featureless face below a mop of dun-colored hair could have belonged to either gender.

"Don't try to move, I'll be there in a minute!" shouted the policeman again.

But his words did not have the desired effect. The small, drab figure crawled back into the shadows of the cave. This, in turn, spurred the young man to greater efforts, and he almost ran into the dark maw in the cliff side.

Mrs. Allington waited, on tenterhooks, for the policeman to emerge with the poor little child in his arms. As seconds turned to minutes, she began to wonder if he had indeed suffered a fall on the slippery rocks. It was hard to imagine any other possibility. She considered calling the police, but had a vague feeling that that could be an offense, given that the police were already present.

"Oh, this is ridiculous!" she said to herself, and began to make her way over the weed-slick rocks.

Behind her, the incoming tide started to wash away all the footprints that had been left in the sand that morning.

* * *

Trick or Treat
By Sara Clancy

We were both well aware that we were too old for trick or treating. But we had three movies left to go in our marathon and the candy had run out. Since Cindy and I were on good terms with all of our neighbors, I figured that we would get something as long as we kept to our street. So, after tossing on some old bedsheets to give the appearance of effort, we set out.

Kids flooded the walkways, moving as a chaotic stream from one house to the next and battering against our legs as they passed. It was still early in the evening, just dark enough to let the decorations shine. The mechanical growls and whirls of the more elaborate setups were barely audible under the delighted squeals as we made our rounds. While just about everyone rolled their eyes at us, they still gave us a handful or two of their candy stash, making it well worth the effort. We had more than enough by the time we had completed the loop and were headed back to our house. That's when I stopped at Mr. Wilson's house.

"I didn't know that he set up a haunted house this year," Cindy said while we paused to let the stream of children pass before us.

Mr. Wilson had never really been into the whole Halloween thing. Not that he ruined the fun for anyone else. Instead, he just skipped town for a few days. I studied the faces of the children as they passed. Apparently, his setup wasn't that great. They weren't laughing with their usual glee. But then, they weren't chatting about how lame it was either. I couldn't decide if that was a good sign or not.

"We should go check it out," I said.

Cindy gave me a sour look. "You wanted to see horror movies, and I gave you that. My charity ends there."

There wasn't a person on earth easier to scare than Cindy. Which of course made her the perfect person to do these sorts of things with. If the place was too lame to offer a thrill, at least I'd have her to laugh at.

"Oops, he's spotted us," I said as I returned his wave. "Can't get out of it now."

Cindy alternated between glaring at me and smiling politely at Mr. Wilson as we headed up the path to his house.

"Trick or treat," we beamed in way of greeting.

We went through the usual remarks as he placed generous handfuls of candy into our bags, but we quickly ran out of things to talk about. So I mentioned his haunted house. Mr. Wilson looked so damn proud of himself that we couldn't say no when he invited us inside.

Cindy kept close to my side as we entered. But the tension in her shoulders soon faded. Dark plastic sheeting had been hung up to close the room off from the others, creating a crude maze. Dime store cobwebs with plastic spiders were tossed over a long, thin table while bedsheets hung from the ceiling, balloons plumping up their insides. Mr. Wilson further ruined any atmosphere as he ran about, organizing his costume and hitting on an old tape player. The sounds of the thunderstorm distorted as the tape struggled to move. Mostly, it just sounded like static.

Cindy and I shared a glance. It seemed like neither of us could decide if it was funny or a little sad. We straightened our features as Mr. Wilson turned around. With his cloak and top hat, I supposed he was going for an old English gentleman vibe. Clicking his fingers like he had just remembered something, he crouched down and pulled a large doll from under the table. It was about the size of a five-year-old. It had a frilly Victorian dress, and its hair was matted, with its skin shining in the dull light.

Mr. Wilson held the doll close to his chest, completely forgetting to turn it around so it was facing us, and waved his free arm out wide.

"Welcome one and all to my, I mean our, haunted house. Oh, right, this is Jessica."

It didn't seem like the arms of the doll could move, so he just sort of popped it from side to side, talking out of the side of his mouth to give it a voice. He still didn't notice that we couldn't see the doll's face. Cindy and I both said 'hello' to the doll in an effort to play along.

Mr. Wilson grinned. "I've been practicing. Bet you didn't see my lips move."

In unison, we lied, agreeing that we had missed the obvious movement. We couldn't bring ourselves to disappoint him. With a flourish of his hand, he took us into the next room. As we walked, he weaved a story about a haunted mansion somewhere in England. It was hard to follow since he forgot more lines than he remembered and was constantly backtracking to correct himself. The next room was just as bad. There were a few rubber bats, a sheet over the window that was already falling down, and a table set with bowls of cold spaghetti and peeled grapes.

Mr. Wilson declared them to be intestines and eyes before realizing that he had forgotten to cover them. He made his apologies, juggling Jessica as he searched for whatever was supposed to be tossed over them. So we politely averted our gazes and give him some time. Cindy gasped sharply and I whipped around to face her. She had one hand on her chest and was trying to catch her breath. Over her shoulder, I saw what had startled her. A mannequin was set against the wall beside the door, dressed in a cheap doctor's costume and its face hidden behind a surgical mask.

"Seriously," I chuckled under my breath.

"I thought someone was standing there," Cindy said just as quietly.

Mr. Wilson recaptured our attention and continued with his

story. I almost groaned as he took it from the top, still weaving the Jessica doll back and forth when he tried to talk for her. Even as boredom began to brew inside me, we made sure to listen patiently, chuckling and gasping at the appropriate moments. The only thing that made it bearable was the way Cindy kept sneaking peeks at the mannequin, like she expected it to move. I nudged her. She was startled just like before, this time turning to glare at me. It improved my mood immensely.

"It's staring at me," she whispered.

"It can't *stare* at anyone. It doesn't have eyes."

It was hard to keep from laughing at her as we followed Mr. Wilson to the next room. His kitchen. Here, two mannequins sat at the kitchen table, each tipping at odd angles like they were about to topple onto the floor. Mr. Wilson rushed over to move them back into place. The movement was clunky, with none of their arms or legs moving at all. Each one had the same lacquered shine as Jessica. Like a well-polished table.

After they were righted, Mr. Wilson began his speech about them summoning forth dark spirits with their Ouija board. It was the same urban legend I'd heard since I was three, so I took to watching Cindy instead. Her nose wrinkled slightly as she sniffed at the air.

"What?" I asked.

"Can't you smell that?" she whispered back.

To humor her, I took a few discrete sniffs. Under the traces of candle smoke, there was a sharp note of chemicals. Not bleach. Something else I hadn't smelled before. I shrugged at her. We were in a kitchen. It wasn't unheard of for someone to go overboard with the antiseptic. Then we were moving again, going into a little offshoot by the laundry room.

The chemical smell grew stronger until it burned my nose. Cindy lifted her hand to cover her mouth. We exchanged a look, but neither of us said anything. There were three mannequins crammed into the small laundry room. They were dressed in cheap clown outfits with a bit of fake blood splattered across the walls, each drop statically placed for an easy clean up off the tiles. The hallway light caught on what little of their body was left uncovered. They each had that same shiny finish, but they seemed to be older, with fine cracks appearing across their 'skin'. Like breaks in a painting. I was trying to pinpoint what that smell was when Mr. Wilson juggled Jessica into his other arm and swept aside the curtain that he had put up to divide the hallway.

The moment the plastic rippled back, a ripe stench wafted out. It mixed with the now ever-present reek of chemicals. The stench was an almost physical thing. I could feel it coating my throat a little more with each breath. Tilting my head to the side, I peered into the darkness and fought down the urge to gag. Cindy clenched my hand as her eyes adjusted enough to see the dozen of cloaked figures. All of their hoods were pulled up, leaving only their frozen, lifeless hands visible.

Mr. Wilson turned on an electronic candle he had fished out of his pocket and held it out so that the light pushed a little into the darkness. The hands glistened as if they were slick.

"This way," Mr. Wilson said in an exaggerated tone.

Cindy's hand squeezed me until it hurt. I was about to pull away when I saw her expression. The color had drained from her face, leaving a slight greenish tinge, and she continued to swallow thickly like she was going to be sick.

"What's in there, Mr. Wilson?" she asked.

He wiggled his fingers. With Jessica in one hand and the candle in the other, it wasn't an easy task.

"All of my victims," he said before breaking into a brilliant smile.

There was something in the expression that made me cringe. It was a knowing little smirk, like a child that had a secret and was waiting with anticipation for the great reveal. I eyed the line-up of figures again. It would be easy to hide a friend in there to jump out at as we passed.

"I meant the smell," Cindy said softly.

Mr. Wilson's smile grew impish. He was almost bouncing on his toes with delight. "You know, I normally preserve them. But some have had the audacity to start rotting anyway. Rude, right? That's alright, though. I'm just going to start again."

I waited for him to look away before I rolled my eyes and leaned closer to Cindy to whisper, "Twenty bucks it's old hamburger meat."

Cindy gave me a sideways look. "I don't like this."

I laughed and nudged her with my elbow. "How can you be scared right now?"

I had to grab her hand to get her moving again. The moment we entered the hallway, the stench became unbearable. Mr. Wilson had really gone overboard. With the mannequins on either side, we had to walk in single file. Cindy squeezed my palm, her grip tightening with every step. Using my other hand to cover my mouth, I tried to pay attention to what Mr. Wilson was saying, but it was a struggle. Every now and then, our leader would look back over his shoulder to check that we were still there. That smile remained on his face the entire time. That secretive, expectant smile. It was starting to get to me. I knew someone was coming. I just didn't know when.

I couldn't take looking at that smile anymore, so I shifted my attention to the figures, sneaking glimpses at their hands and what little of their faces I could make out. Their fingernails were black. Not black nail polish, but a rotten, molten black that pressed up under the outline of the nails. Almost like a bruise. It was an astonishing amount of detail to give to something so pointless. It must have taken him hours to perfect. I couldn't pinpoint why, but it bothered me.

I was grateful when we finally reached the end of the hallway and passed through the next curtain of plastic sheeting. The smell remained. Like it had seeped into my pores and coated my hair. There was no ignoring it, and I had to swallow a few times to keep myself from being sick. Cindy pressed close to my side, not faring much better.

"And now, for the end of my tour," Mr. Wilson said with glee.

He reached down, placing the electronic candle on the floor in favor of grabbing a small metal ring. One pull and a whine of hinges had the basement door opened. Cindy grabbed my wrist and pulled me closer. We quickly exchanged a look before studying the opening. There wasn't a hint of light, leaving the trapdoor as little more than a gaping pit. I strained to hear the slightest bit of movement. The setting was just too perfect for a jump scare. It took me a second to realize that, no matter how hard I strained, I couldn't hear a thing beyond the soft murmur of the tape recording. Even the sounds of the kids outside were gone.

"Watch your step," Mr. Wilson grinned.

I looked from him to the pit. Then smirked over my shoulder at Cindy. "You first."

"I don't want to go down there," she whispered.

Mr. Wilson stepped forward before I had a chance to tease her, thrusting little Jessica out before him.

"You're scared? Here, take her with you. She was really brave."

Cindy reluctantly released her death grip on my arm and accepted the doll. She took to fussing over it as a way to calm her nerves. Making sure the dress was sitting just right and trying to fix her hair. I turned back to Mr. Wilson. He was still grinning, but not at me. His eyes were on Cindy and Jessica. For the longest time, he didn't seem to breathe or move or blink. I was completely forgotten.

"So," I said to break the silence. "I guess I'm first."

Mr. Wilson snapped out of his daze. With a wide wave of his arms, he beckoned me closer. I took one step before Cindy's arm latched onto my wrist again. She was doubled over by the time I turned around, her hair sweeping down to cover her face. Jessica clattered against the floorboards as Cindy gagged. From my position just next to her, I could make out the tiniest slither of her face. Just enough to see her jab a few fingers down her throat. From Mr. Wilson's position, it would most likely look like she was trying to stop herself from vomiting instead of inducing it.

Before I could ask her what the hell she was doing, a violent tremble ran through her body. She squeezed my wrist until I was sure the bone would crack, then vomit gushed from her mouth. The sight and smell were almost enough to take me go over the edge with her. I tried to pull away as she repeated the process to make herself sick again.

"Cindy!" I snapped as a bit of bile splashed on my shoes. "What the hell?"

"I'm sorry," she mumbled, lifting her head just enough to glance at Mr. Wilson. "I think it's all the candy. And the smell. I'm sorry, I should go home."

The words left her mouth so fast that they almost bled together. The way she sounded made it harder for me to be mad at her.

"Sorry 'bout this, Mr. Wilson," I said as I rubbed Cindy's back in soothing circles. "I'll take her home and then come back to clean this up."

Tiny droplets of blood welled up along my forearm as Cindy dug her nails in. I hissed in pain but helped her to stand.

"You'll be back?" Mr. Wilson asked.

His unblinking stare sent a shiver down my spine. I nodded slightly. "Yeah. I'll just get her to bed first."

Mr. Wilson stepped forward and Cindy inched back. Somehow, his grin stretched even further as he picked up Jessica and held her out in front of him.

"Why don't you take her? She likes you."

"No," Cindy stammered quickly. "Thank you. You'll need her for your next trick or treaters."

I didn't have time to even shoot her a strange look before she started pulling at my arm. A few muttered threats that she was about to be sick again finally got me to stop resisting. We hurried down the hallway, back through the kitchen and living room, and out the front door. Only once we were crossing the yard did she let go of me and break into a flat out run. I glanced over my shoulder to see Mr. Wilson standing on the porch, holding Jessica, ghastly smile still in place. I shrugged at him before I began running to catch up with Cindy.

She was through the front door of the house before I had even made it up the driveway.

"What is going on?" I said as I crossed the threshold.

Cindy was in the kitchen, phone pressed to her ear and knife in her free hand.

"Lock the door," she hissed.

The fear in her voice made me act instantly. We had locked all of the other doors before we had left, so I had expected the click of the lock to offer her some comfort. It didn't. Without turning on a light, she pressed her back to the wall, sliding down to pull herself into a tight ball.

"Who are you calling?"

Cindy shushed me and her call connected. The green light cast deep shadows over her face and left me uneasy

"Hello?" she whispered.

Her eyes darted around as she waved for me to sit down next to her. I could hear the muffled voice on the other end of the line but couldn't make out the words. It wasn't until Cindy was giving our address, as well as Mr. Wilson's, that it clicked. She had called the police.

"What are you doing?" I hissed.

She ignored me. "You need to send someone straight away. My neighbor has the girl that went missing. The one on the news last night."

I was too shocked to respond. My mouth gaped as she continued in a rush.

"No, he's preserved her somehow. He's using her like a doll. No, no, I held her in my hands. I saw her face. Her skin chipped away in my hands. I saw bone. It wasn't a doll!"

All of her words jumbled over each other as they entered my ears. I just couldn't wrap my head around it. Mr. Wilson had been our neighbor for years.

"I think there are others," Cindy whimpered. "The mannequins had fingernails. Eyelashes. Please, just hurry. He tried to get us into his basement. No, we're at home now. I tried to cover but I think he knows."

He knows. The thought lodged into my brain. It was chased quickly by another thought. We house-sit for each other. I strained, pushing through the chaos filling my mind, but I couldn't remember if I had gotten the spare set of keys back from him. A creak of the porch floorboard made my heart stop. I grabbed Cindy's hand and pulled her to her feet. There was no time to get out the back door so I opened the crawlspace under the stairs and shoved her through. The sound of keys clicking together made Cindy's feet falter. By the glow of the phone, I saw her eyes widen. I hurled myself in after her. There was barely enough room for the both of us and our legs pressed together painfully as I hooked my fingers under the door and pulled it shut.

Cindy opened her mouth to say something, but the whisper of hinges kept her silent. Sitting in the dark, with both breaths held, alert to every slight groan and creak. The voices of children grew and fell swiftly. It took me half a second to figure out why. The door had opened and closed. Someone was inside the house. The footsteps slow, steady. As if trying to minimize any noise. I could only faintly hear them as they trailed up the stairs above our heads. Cindy was shaking. I could see it by the tremble of the phone light that she was trying to smother against her cheek.

"He's here," she whispered to the person on the other end of the line.

The call seemed at once, both a protection and completely useless. Hot tears trickled from my eyes as I listened for more footsteps, desperately trying to place where he was. Mr. Wilson barely offered a sound. To the point that it seemed he was everywhere and nowhere at once. The moment I was sure he was in the upstairs bathroom, I would catch the soft scrape of shoes over the kitchen tiles. The backdoor would rattle but shadows would slip through the light seeping under the door.

I almost screamed when the voice called to us. Not Mr. Wilson's real voice. The one he had used for Jessica. High-pitched and taunting, followed by a giggle that set my nerves on end. He called to us in that voice over and over, trying to coax us out. Cindy flicked against me when we heard cupboard doors violently ripping open. He was looking for us. We both looked to the little door of the crawlspace. The only way I could keep it closed from inside was to slip my fingers through the gap and tug. Images flooded my head of a knife stabbing under the door and severing my fingers should I try.

My mind whirled, trying to think up what I'd do if the door opened. There wasn't any room to move. I didn't have a weapon. The footsteps drew nearer, slowed, and stopped just inches from our hiding place. Mr. Wilson spoke again, keeping to that twisted, childish voice that I could have sworn was coming from right beside me. Like he was lurking in the darkness with us.

Police sirens pierced the night. I never heard Mr. Wilson leave. Neither Cindy nor I dared to breathe until we heard the police entering the front door. We didn't move until the voice on the other end of the line said it was safe. Slowly, we crept from our hiding place and into the waiting arms of a police officer. It was a moment of chaos. With the officers trying to get us outside as swiftly as possible. The strain on their faces told me that Mr. Wilson hadn't been caught yet. But it was what I spotted as they nearly dragged us outside that made me think they weren't going to find him.

Jessica stood only a few feet from the hatch we had been hiding in. Her mangled hair was pushed back, allowing me to see the grotesque rot that Cindy had seen before. A note was written across the front of her dress. Three simple words that meant nothing, but promised so much.

Trick or treat.

* * *

The Steak House
By Ron Ripley

"The stuff's still in there," Becky said, her hands cupped around the side of her face as she peered into one of the back windows.

Howie flicked the butt of his cigarette into the sewer grate, grinned at the spray of embers from the burning tobacco, and said, "What stuff, and why the hell do you want to go in there?"

Becky turned around, brushed a stray forelock of pink hair back and winked at him. "Did you see the taxidermy in there?"

"The what?" he asked.

Becky sighed and shook her head. "I forget how stupid you are. The deer heads and stuff on the walls."

"I'm not stupid," Howie grumbled, walking up to the back window. He used his hands to block out the cold, fluorescent light of the parking lot's lamps and squinted. In the gloom of the abandoned restaurant's dining area, he saw the deer heads.

Four of them, maybe more. It was hard to tell with all of the shadows. A glance at the ceiling showed three large chandeliers hanging down, each one made from twenty or thirty sets of antlers. Along the walls were pictures of cowboys, even some hats hung above the booths. Big old, wide-brimmed hats just like John Wayne used to wear in the Westerns.

"Damn," Howie said, nodding appreciatively.

"Right?" Becky grinned at him, played with the gauge in her left ear and asked, "So, want to go in and see what we can get?"

Howie glanced around, saw a couple of teens walking into the Denny's Restaurant across the lot and asked, "Think we can do it?"

She rolled her eyes and said, "Howie, it's two thirty in the morning. There's not going to be a better time."

He thought about it for a moment, scratched the back of his head and asked, "Think it's got an alarm?"

"No," Becky said, and he heard the exasperation in her voice. He didn't care though. He was the one on parole for assault, not Becky.

"Listen," she said, a playful, pouting tone replacing the frustration, "the place has been empty for three years, which means it won't even have electricity."

"You sure?" Howie asked, shooting a furtive look at the building.

"I'm sure," she purred. "My dad's a contractor, remember? When a place gets shut down like this, banks send in guys like my dad to 'winterize' it. That means the water gets shut down, all the pipes drained. Nobody's paying the gas bill or the electric bill, or anything, so everything's shut off. Worst thing we'll find in there are probably some traps."

Howie still wasn't convinced. Something was off about the place, and he didn't like it.

All of those concerns vanished though as Becky pressed close to him, her breath hot against his ear as she whispered, "And we'll be alone."

Howie smiled and nodded.

Taking her by the hand, he led Becky to the rear entrance. Tall shrubs had grown over the small walkway, and the shadows around the door offered a place to hide from any prying eyes if someone should drive by.

Howie dug his phone out of his pocket, hit the flashlight and held the phone up so he could see what the door looked like.

"Holy crap," he muttered, "looks like we're not the first ones."

A pry-bar lay on the concrete walkway. Dirty, orange rust stains spread out from the tool. It had been weeks since the last heavy rain, and the bar looked as though it had lain there for a lot longer than that. The door itself wasn't closed all the way, almost a quarter of an inch of it was past the framework.

Howie only hesitated for a moment before he took hold of the handle and eased the door back.

The hinges screamed in protest, metal grinding against metal. He winced, heart racing as he pulled the door back far enough for the two of them to slip into the abandoned restaurant.

As he stood just inside the doorway, his nose wrinkled and he fought back the urge to gag. A rank, fetid odor filled the air. It was as if someone had left a dumpster full of rotting food baking in the August sun, and then dumped the contents in the restaurant.

"God," he complained, "this place stinks."

"Grow up," Becky said, slapping him on the arm as she passed by.

A long, low groan sounded from the far left, silencing any comeback Howie could have offered.

"What the hell was that?" he demanded, twisting toward the sound.

"What was what?" Becky shot back over her shoulder, maneuvering through the dining room. At the few tables in the room's center, the chairs had been upended and stacked on top, as if waiting for the morning crew to come in and clean the floors. The thick layer of dust showed that the restaurant was waiting in vain.

Howie shined the light on the floor, looking at the animal tracks that cut through the dust, trying to see where exactly the noise had come from.

"Put the light out!" Becky snapped. "Do you want someone to notice us?"

Howie rolled his eyes, but he turned off the light, stuffing his phone into his back pocket.

"So," Becky said, flashing him a smile, "which one do you think I should take home?"

"I don't know," he grumbled. "Just pick one. I don't like it in here."

"What?" Becky asked, snickering. "Are you afraid of the dark, Howie?"

"No," he said, "I just don't like it in here."

A groan came out of the darkness at the far end of the room.

"Holy crap," Becky hissed, "is someone here?"

"I don't know," Howie whispered, suddenly sweating. "Let's just get the hell out of here."

She shook her head. "No. We should make them get out. I want those damned heads."

"Are you out of your mind?" Howie demanded.

Becky glared at him. "I want a head. I am not leaving without one."

With that, she turned her back on him and walked across the floor.

"Hey," she said, her voice low and threatening, "whoever's in here, you need to get the hell out, understand? This is my place now."

No one answered her. She glanced over her shoulder at Howie, but he only shrugged.

"You better come with me!" she whispered fiercely.

Howie's shoulders sagged as he followed her towards the darkness.

"Answer me!" Becky said, raising her voice a few octaves higher.

A long, low moan was the only response given, and Howie saw her become tense. He knew that her temper was rising, that her anger would get the better of her, and that the situation was going to get worse in a matter of moments.

"God damn it," Becky snarled, her Doc Martens boots thudding on the restaurant's worn floor.

Howie glanced around, a sense of unease growing. "Becky."

"Shut it," she hissed at him. To the stranger in the darkness, she said, "Come out!"

No one came out of the shadows.

As they approached the far end of the restaurant, the stench they had first encountered grew stronger.

"God, Becky," Howie coughed, gagging, "this place stinks. I think somebody might have died in here."

"Yeah, maybe the person who's hiding killed them," she said, her voice thick with sarcasm. "It's just rotting food or something. Get over it."

Before Howie could protest, she raised her voice again to the unseen squatter.

"Listen," she commanded, "if you're not out of here in thirty seconds, we're going to drag you out and beat you up."

Something wet and heavy was dragged across the floor, the sound both irritating and frightening.

"That's it," Becky fumed. "They've had enough time. Give me your light."

Howie didn't bother arguing. He pulled his phone back out, switched the flashlight on and handed the phone to her.

Becky swung the phone up, shining it down at an angle. The light it cast was bright and harsh, yet it couldn't penetrate to the far wall, which was less than twenty feet away. She muttered something about Howie buying cheap electronics and walked forward. Howie followed close behind her, not wanting to be too far away. He glanced at the walls and the windows, wondering how much force it would take to break the glass if they had to get out in a hurry.

"What the hell?" Becky asked, coming to a sharp stop.

Howie almost bumped into her but managed to twist away in time. As he regained his balance, he looked at the back wall, tried to understand what Becky was concerned about, and then he saw it.

A large, black stain spread across the lower third of the wood-paneled wall. In the cone of the phone's light, the darkness had no form, no definition. It wasn't a wall hidden in shadow. The wood hadn't been painted black.

There was nothing to be seen. Nothing to touch.

But even as he looked at it, Howie understood that the lower portion of the wall pulsed. It moved in an erratic rhythm that caused him to shake.

"I think we should go," Howie whispered, and his words were punctuated by a long, low growl that coincided with the curious, wet dragging sound they had heard a minute before.

"Yeah," Becky whispered, all of the bravado gone from her voice. She took a step back, and Howie screamed.

A long tendril of shadow shot out of the darkness with a horrifying, numbing speed. Unable to close his eyes against the sight, Howie watched as the dark limb lashed out, snapping and coiling around his thigh. His eyes widened, and a heartbeat later he screamed again, a sound of surprise mingled with pain and terror.

Howie felt himself jerked back with all of the morbid grace of a fish on a hook. His phone fell from Becky's hand, clattering against the floor, the light shining up at the ceiling.

More tendrils spat out of the shadow on the wall as Howie screamed her name.

But Becky did nothing.

She stood and watched, a look of curiosity and mild fascination on her face.

For a fleeting moment, rage replaced Howie's fear, and he screamed at her.

Becky's response was a smirk, and before he could let loose his fury, he felt a terrible, sharp pain.

Slowly, from the ceiling, long shadows unfurled. Hundreds of dark tendrils snapped out, racing towards him.

Howie tried to run, to rip away the thick limb wrapped around his own, but Becky pushed him back. He slammed into a table, knocked the upended chairs down and hit the floor hard enough to crack his teeth together. Pain exploded in his jaw, and he knew something had broken, but fear drove him back to his feet, pushed him forward.

It wasn't enough.

The first of the tendrils pierced his clothes, hidden barbs digging into his skin and dragging him to a stop.

"Help me!" he screamed.

Becky shook her head, a small, pleased smile on her face.

"Becky!" Howie begged.

"No," she said unsympathetically. "It's hungry, and It needs to eat."

Howie shrieked and clawed at her as she deftly stepped out of reach.

He tripped, and as he hit the wood, he felt thousands of needles puncture his flesh. They tore into his arms and legs, buried themselves into his back and chest. Dug into his stomach and neck. Howie opened his mouth to beg, and more tendrils raced into his throat, pulling at the soft flesh of his cheeks and shredding his tongue.

All that slipped free from him was a long, plaintive moan, one that filled the restaurant as he was pulled backward. A hideous trio of tongues, barbed and glistening in the light, slapped out onto the floor, creating a low, wet, dragging sound as they reached for Howie. The air became moist and foul, and the last rational thought he had was the understanding that the shadow on the wall was a mouth, and he was being dragged into it.

* * *

Thunder Run
By David Longhorn

"Isn't it amazing?" asked Lamkin. "That he trod these very boards?"

Strode glanced at the fat little man in bemusement, tinged with annoyance. He looked down at the uneven boards beneath their feet. The stage of the theater was much like any other, as far as he could see.

"Sorry," said Strode, "who we talking about again?"

Lamkin looked hurt as well as nervous, eyes wide in a face glistening with sweat.

"Why, Stan Laurel, of course!"

"Stuart is very keen on Laurel and Hardy," put in Doctor Mountford, the other trustee.

"Oh, right," said Strode, turning away from the pair and taking another look around the stage. "Theater history, fascinating I'm sure."

Outside the Adelphi Theater, posters advertised tribute bands to acts that had been big in the Eighties, plus a few upcoming concerts by actual bands that had been big in the Seventies. Comedians were also featured prominently, but there were no real big names. Mostly acts that had been big in the Nineties. Rather optimistically, given that it was only June, the Adelphi was also inviting people to buy tickets to the Christmas pantomime. Snow White, it was, starring some reality show winner and some pouting nonentity from a third-rate girl-band. And now Lamkin was trying to persuade him that the Adelphi was a going concern that just needed a little cash injection. Trying to make Strode fall in love with the place.

Pathetic, thought Strode, as he assessed just how long it would take to demolish the place. *A business dying on its feet, and all this idiot can talk about is history.*

"I don't think Mister Strode is keen on showbiz nostalgia," said Doctor Mountford. "He is a man of business, after all."

"Yeah, right," said Strode, looking at the woman dubiously. When he had heard that one of the trustees of the theater was a woman, he had anticipated a bit of banter, maybe a pat on the backside and some post-meeting fun in his hotel room. But when he met Isadora, all thoughts of fun fled. She was one of those arty women with no posterior to pat; just a lot of skin and bone seemingly held together with ethnic jewelry. The other trustee, Lamkin, was a typical enthusiast, the sort who volunteered for charity. Strode despised them both, but was careful not to show it.

"So it's a very old building," he said. "And costly to maintain. That's why I think you should accept my offer, as you won't get a better one. And of course it's a time-limited offer. If you turn me down and then change your mind, the price I'm prepared to pay goes down."

"Oh, we're very interested," burbled Lamkin. "It came as quite a surprise to find that a property developer like yourself could take an interest in our theatrical heritage."

I'm interested in money, you idiot, thought Strode. *Something you and your board seem to be singularly unable to make.*

"We can cut the tour short now," said Mountford. "I'm sure Mister Strode has a very tight schedule."

First sensible thing anyone's said since I got here.

"Yeah, right," he said. "I just needed to see the place in person. Never delegate the important stuff, that's my motto."

"Very wise," said Mountford.

"You're sure you don't want to see our extensive collection of Victorian posters?" asked Lamkin, plaintively.

Strode, struggling to keep his temper, said, "No thank you, I have a flight back to London at—"

Then he stopped, turned, stared at a corner of the stage. There was nothing there. But Strode was sure he had seen a flurry of movement. Perhaps it was a shadow cast by someone dodging into the wings. Strode had a deep aversion to anyone overhearing his business talks and insisted that they never be recorded.

"Something wrong?" asked Mountford. All three were now looking to the left of the stage.

"No, no," said Strode, "I just thought I saw something. Hey, what is that thing?"

He pointed to an odd-looking wooden chute that emerged from the wall. It was in the area where he thought he had seen movement, and Strode felt a sudden unaccountable urge to know more about it.

"Ah," said Mountford. "The thunder run. Stuart is the man to tell you about that."

"Yes, indeed!" enthused Lamkin. "It's a fascinating example of a nineteenth century stage effect. You see, drama at the time often required blood and thunder, and not metaphorically. Stage blood was easily done, but thunder took more effort."

The little man turned to gesture out from the stage at the semi-circular auditorium.

"The thunder run is a chute that passes behind the wall, around the entire theater, spiraling downwards. When a storm was needed, as in King Lear for instance, a series of six-pound cannonballs were deposited at the top of the run and thundered along behind the audience, creating a splendid effect."

"And that's where the cannonballs came out?" asked Strode, pointing. "Didn't they damage the stage?"

"They landed on sandbags," put in Mountford. "And were then gathered up by a young apprentice stagehand, who climbed a ladder and put them back in at the top of the run again."

Mountford indicated a place high above the right side of the stage. Strode could just make out the beginning of the chute.

"Okay," he said, "quite a nice anecdote for the guys at the golf club. Thanks!"

"Oh, that's not the main story," said Mountford, with an odd smile. "Stuart, you should tell him, it's your pet obsession."

Strode looked at Lamkin, who seemed to be sweating even more, seemed to hesitate.

"Perhaps I'd better explain," said the woman. "The theater is supposed to be haunted by the ghost of a boy who died working the thunder run."

Ghosts! Now I've heard it all, thought Strode. *These people are going to be a pushover.*

"Tell me more," he said, faking enthusiasm.

"The boy, named Tommy, had to put the cannonballs in the run, slide down the ladder, then run behind the backdrop to collect them," explained Mountford. "One night Tommy tripped, fell headlong into the sandbags. Just as the first ball came out of the run."

Strode had a sudden vision of the accident, could even hear a boyish cry of despair as the apprentice fell. Then he heard the sickening crunch, saw blood and brains spill onto the sandbags and the gas lit boards, heard the absurd, inevitable cry go up.

"Is there a doctor in the house?"

"What?" asked Lamkin. "I didn't quite catch that?"

Did I say that aloud? Must be letting these idiots get to me, thought Strode. He was shocked at how undisciplined his imagination had become all of a sudden. Normally his mind could be relied upon to focus on business, or the various forms of pleasure his wealth bought him.

"Nothing," he said. "Cool story, but I must be going. As I said, the formal offer for the site will be with you before the weekend, and—"

He stopped, seeing Lamkin's aghast expression, Mountford's cynical smile.

Shit, he thought, *I've done it now. Letting a bloody ghost story rattle me like that!*

"Site?" asked Lamkin. "Did you say site?"

"Mister Strode is a developer," purred the woman. "That means he knocks down old buildings, puts up new ones."

Strode took a deep breath. He had hoped to simply check out the structure and avoid any unpleasantness.

"Quite," he said. "I'm buying up properties on both sides of Eastgate Road so as to create a retail hub. And that means a big car park. This site, plus the ones to either side, seem ideal for that purpose."

Lamkin turned red and started spluttering, struggling to form words. But Mountford was, as always, ready with an articulate response.

"Mister Lamkin and the other trust members thought you were offering to revitalize the Adelphi," she said. "Your approach was worded rather ambiguously."

Her tone called Strode a liar, a con-artist.

"Well, I'm sorry you feel that way," snapped the businessman. "Because I've got quite a reputation for regenerating run-down areas like this. And before you tell me about this building's heritage, let me tell you something. Heritage, of itself, doesn't make money. You can talk about Stan Laurel, sure, but when we came in, I didn't see a single product on sale in the foyer with his face on it."

"But this is such a vital link to the past—" began Lamkin.

Strode cut him off with a peremptory gesture and started to walk offstage.

"The people who built this place wanted to make money, not establish a glorified museum! Anyway, the new complex will include a multi-screen cinema, something people will actually pay good money to enjoy. Unlike this old relic—"

Strode stopped, again taken off guard. The vibration coming through the floorboards was subsonic at first, but then entered his hearing range as a rumbling that seemed to circle the old building. Mountford and Lamkin were also frozen to the spot. The fat little trustee looked stressed enough to have a stroke. Mountford, to Strode's surprise, had lost her cynical smile and seemed to have turned a shade paler.

The vibration ended, and they all looked at the end of the thunder run. Nothing emerged from the wooden chute. After a moment's silence, Strode gave a laugh.

"Well, this place will fall down of its own accord if they keep running twenty ton trucks past it! Those old Victorians never saw that coming, eh?"

Lamkin scurried after Strode, trying to make him change his mind and become a 'friend of the Adelphi'.

"I'm quite happy to remain an acquaintance, thanks," retorted Strode.

Mountford, bringing up the rear, said nothing until Strode climbed into his rental car. She leaned down and spoke through the driver's window.

"I know I won't dissuade you from knocking down the Adelphi," she said. "Your sort are always sure of yourselves."

Starting up the Lexus, Strode looked out at her and raised an eyebrow.

"I'm sensing a 'but', Doctor Mountford, so get it over with."

"Very well," she said. "People who are, let us say, not friends of the Adelphi are said to incur the wrath of the ghost. Tommy is said to preside over productions at the theater. He can be a bit mischievous if anyone tries to undermine a production—a diva refusing to go on, that kind of thing. The show must go on, seems to be his motto. Who knows how he might react to someone seeking to stop the show forever?"

"Oh, right," sneered Strode. "And what will the brainless boy do? Bleed on me?"

Before she could reply, he screeched off into the afternoon traffic, blaring his horn at a van driver who did not give way quickly enough.

As he headed for the airport, Strode tried to shed his irritation by reflecting on how well he had done. He now knew that the trustees were going to be a pushover. Why, only two of the nine had even bothered to turn up! If only he had not made that slip over his demolition plans. Still, that nonsense about the ghost would be a good one to tell the lads in the golf club bar. His like-minded friends shared his jovial contempt for artsy-fartsy types. He was so busy trying to find his way through the labyrinthine streets of the unfamiliar city that he did not even see the object before it struck. He felt it, though. The impact struck the offside front wing of the Lexus with a noise like a small bomb going off. He felt the shock through the wheel, and the seat. Swerving to the curb and swearing profusely, he got out to check the damage.

Bang goes my security deposit, he thought. The object, whatever it was, had produced a dent three inches deep and twice as wide. Strode looked around, saw a group of teenage boys standing on a corner about ten yards away. He glared at them as one pointed, said something, and aroused general laughter.

Little bastards! Chucking rocks at luxury motors out of envy. Some time in the army is what they need. Teach 'em discipline!

Strode was about to start remonstrating with the youths when he reflected that starting a fight in a strange neighborhood was never wise. Also, he had to take into account the time needed to sort out the car rental, now that it was damaged. He never lost a deposit if he could help it, but this one would be tricky.

Muttering obscenities, Strode got back into the car and drove away. He glanced back once, to see that the group of lads had moved on. Then he realized that one had stayed behind, loitering on the corner. The teenager was dressed drably, except for what looked like an odd red and white hat of some kind.

What is he wearing? Not a baseball cap, certainly.

Then the road curved away and Strode could no longer see the boy.

"Provincials!" he snorted, focusing once more on the road ahead.

***

Two years passed. Two years during which Strode never returned to the city of Newcastle, instead delegating the Eastgate road project to a succession of underlings. It proved even more troublesome than he had anticipated. There was local opposition against the demolition of the Adelphi, of course, and this proved more stubborn than expected. But even when demolition work began, there were unaccountable delays, with a high turnover of personnel and a series of bad accidents on the site.

Some of his directors even hinted that Strode should go and sort things out in person. Strode retorted that he had a lot of irons in the fire and simply hadn't time to supervise every one. An underling then unwisely pointed out that Strode frequently took his current girlfriend to New York for the weekend. Strode fired the man on the spot, gave him no reference.

But it was not pressure from work that aged Strode during those two years. It was the nightmares. They always began in the same way, with the two trustees showing him around the Adelphi. As they approached the stage, Strode felt mounting apprehension, knowing that something bad was imminent, but never being sure what was coming.

"And it was here that the lovable, gentle silent movie clown Stan Laurel had his head smashed in," said Lamkin. "Skull reduced to pulpy fragments, blood and gray matter splashing out across the stage, staining the dresses of the ladies in the front row."

"No, that can't be right," Strode always replied. "That's just crazy."

"I'm afraid that is the case," said Mountford. "Breaking open a living human skull is always a crowd-pleaser, however vulgar one might find such spectacles. And remember, it's so very profitable! You can't argue with free enterprise. Can you?"

Then the trustees seized him by the arms and dragged him over the end of the thunder run, forced his head down onto the bare, splintered boards. As the rumbling vibrating grew, he heard a vast, unseen audience behind him start to cheer, whoop, whistle. The thunder grew to fill his dream-world.

And then he always woke up, sweating profusely. If he was not alone, his partner would ask what was wrong, and he would say, 'Nothing, go back to sleep'. He would lie awake until the gray light of dawn gave him reason to get up and go to work. And every day he worked with the knowledge that the nightmare would come again.

Then came the call. His site manager reached out, interrupting an important Skype conference with his European partners. Furious at this breach of protocol, it took Strode several minutes to grasp what he was being told.

"Boss, we can't open the car park tomorrow," said Gary Marlow. His voice quavered, knowing that he was flirting with career suicide. "No way can it be ready in time."

"What the hell do you mean?" roared Strode. "I put you in charge to get it done on time. You're my troubleshooter. Now you tell me you've shot yourself in your own bollocks!"

He was pacing up and down in his office at his country house, knowing that his underlings called him 'the caged panther' when he was in one of these rages. He liked the nickname, but his doctor had told him to ease up on the tantrums. Remembering this, he stopped pacing and looked out of the French windows onto the lawn. Someone moved, ducking behind an ornamental hedge. Frowning, he tried to see if it was an interloper or just one of his groundskeepers. He leaned forward, staring.

"Boss," Marlow was pleading, "I did my best. I paid them way over the going rate and turned a blind eye when they took shortcuts with the small stuff. I told them they'd get a huge bonus if the complex was ready in time. But no dice. I could never get a big enough crew together. They kept getting spooked. It's like the business with the crane, you can't hush things up."

"Crane?" asked Strode. "What are you talking about?"

"There was an accident in the first few weeks, boss," explained Marlow. "Don't know the details. Just know a wrecking ball fell on this guy. Somehow the chain broke just before they were going to smash in the facade of the old theater."

"I don't recall that," said Strode, puzzled, his temper starting to subside. Again, he caught a hint of movement by the shrubbery.

A boy? Or a girl, maybe. Somebody on the small side, anyway.

"There was an investigation and a report by the Health and Safety Inspectorate," insisted Marlow. "Maybe you were too busy to notice?"

"Right, right," said Strode impatiently.

Now he remembered the incident. There had been a fuss in the national press, questions asked by snooping journalists, libelous claims made on social media. He ignored it all, and it had blown over. His dozen or so projects had frequent accidents. It was impossible to remember them all.

"Or did you just want to forget that particular mishap?"

The voice sounded in his ear, but not one to which he had pressed his phone. It was a quiet, breathy voice. Not that of an adult, he thought. Strode scanned the room but he was alone. A tiny voice came from his cell.

"Boss?" asked Marlow. "I was saying, if you come up here, I could show you—"

"I haven't got time to come up there!" bellowed Strode.

"City planning department say they won't sign off on the shopping mall if we can't provide adequate parking," said Marlow in an even voice. "They want you to sort it out in person."

Strode would normally have erupted in fury at that kind of bureaucratic stonewalling. But somehow, the anger would not come this time. Instead, he looked out at the garden again, hoping to glimpse the boy or girl. Hoping for proof that the small, drab-clad figure was definitely outside.

"Boss?" Marlow sounded puzzled, anxious, perhaps wondering if Strode had finally had the stroke the entire board of directors had long expected.

"Okay, Gary," said Strode evenly. "I get the picture. I'll be there tomorrow; book me a car and a hotel."

He ended the call and then tried to resume his Skype conference. Unfortunately, the time difference meant that the Italians had already gone home. Discussions had to be postponed.

"Lazy Mediterranean bastards," growled Strode as he left his office and went into the palatial living room. "No wonder the Roman Empire collapsed."

"What is it, babe?" said Chantal, his latest paramour. She was draped on the couch leafing through a fashion magazine. A Bengal cat dozed on the floor at her feet.

"Nothing, sugar baps," he replied, throwing himself down next to her. The cat woke up at the noise of him hitting the springs, looked up with huge golden eyes. There was no love lost between Strode and the pet.

"I have to go up to Newcastle," he said, nuzzling up to Chantal and stroking her hair. "I know, I promised you Paris, and we will go! But not this weekend. You'll have to be content with London for another week."

The young woman made a wry face, then kissed him.

"I think we can forgive Daddy this time, can't we, kitten?"

Chantal scratched the cat between its ears. The animal purred, closed its eyes, and suddenly stiffened. It got up and stalked across the room, staring at the door to Strode's office.

"What is it, Lulu?" asked Chantal, sitting up and disengaging Strode's hand from her left breast.

"Bloody animal's crazy," grumbled Strode.

"Lulu?"

Chantal tried to grab the cat, but it had already dashed under the Regency sideboard. It hissed and spat when the woman tried to coax it out.

"The expensive ones are all overbred," grumbled Strode. "Like those yappy little handbag dogs. They're stupid, unreliable."

"Shut your big fat cake-hole!" snapped Chantal. "You always upset her, she's very sensitive. Like me."

Strode began to make placatory noises, but it was too late. His girlfriend left the room, heading for the front door, and he recognized the signs. The slam of the front door was followed by the sound of a Porsche Boxster starting up, the clash of ineptly-handled gears.

Major shopping outbreak, Strode thought. *All my credit cards left severely battered.*

Sighing, he decided to return to his office. But as he reached to open the door, he heard a noise from the other side. It was an exclamation of despair, followed by a sickening thud. Then silence. It took him several seconds to summon up the courage to open the door, and when he did, he flung it wide open like a TV cop on a raid.

Nobody there, of course.

"I'm hearing things," he said. "That bloody woman planted an idea in my head. Stress did the rest."

"Talking to yourself?"

The voice was so close, the speaker had to be behind him. Spinning around, Strode saw nothing living but the Bengal cat, jade eyes staring from the shadows.

"Oh, piss off!" he shouted. "Even if you are a ghost, you don't scare me! Go and haunt somebody else, some pansy actor! Make them piss their pants. You don't scare me at all!"

He turned on his heel to walk back to his desk and saw a drably-clad figure staring into the room. The boy was about ten with huge, dark eyes. Strode felt his heart pounding, heard a distant roar like a waterfall getting louder. He felt himself falling, the world receding as if he had plummeted into a deep well.

***

"There's nothing wrong with me, discussion over!" bellowed Strode as Gary Marlow started to ask him how he was.

"But, boss," Marlow persisted. "Maybe I should drive you into town. Just in case."

"It was not a stroke, just a minor seizure brought on by too much work," said Strode, snapping his fingers.

Reluctantly, Marlow handed over the keys to a silver BMW. As Strode drove them into Newcastle, he fired off a string of questions. By the time they had arrived at Eastgate Road, Strode had arrived to the conclusion that he was one of the few true grown-ups alive in the world today.

Most of them are just kids, he thought. *No guts, scared of their own shadows, easily fooled by daft stories. No wonder I always win.*

"So they all ran away because of this ghost?" asked Strode,

cutting into Marlow's long, rambling account of the last and greatest delay.

"Yes, boss," said Marlow meekly. "There were noises, things were seen."

"You see 'em?"

Marlow could not meet his boss's gaze, stared out at the facade of the new shopping mall.

"I saw something I can't explain. And the noises—"

"Just shut up before I give you your cards!" grated Strode. "Right, let's have a look at the haunted car park, shall we?"

The BMW swung onto the ramp down into the Brutalist concrete structure, taking them out of the autumn sunshine into chilling shadow. Marlow grew quiet, shrank down in his seat, started to play nervously with his tie.

"Stop fidgeting!" snapped Strode. "We've got an appointment with that old bag, the trustee woman. Do you want to look weak in front of some kind of intellectual? Those wankers despise people like us, the wealth creators! We need to show them how strong we are."

Marlow sat up a little straighter, locked his fingers together in his lap. But Strode saw perspiration running down his subordinate's forehead, despite the coolness of the vast underground space.

Isadora Mountford was leaning against her tiny Fiat on the lowest level. Strode pulled up alongside her. Out of habit, he angled the big car so that it almost covered two spaces. When Strode got out, Marlow stayed put in the passenger seat.

"Doctor, good of you to come," said Strode, not offering to shake hands. Instead, he took a gun fighting stance, legs apart, in front of the academic. "I want you to settle a little dispute I've been having with my boy here."

Strode jerked his head back at the BMW.

"I don't have time for games, Mister Strode," said Mountford. "Why did you summon me to this monstrosity?"

"To help lay a ghost!" replied Strode. He raised his arms and turned to face away from the woman, yelling out into the shadowy void. "To tell little Tommy to get stuffed!"

Mountford snorted delicately. But her hands, like Marlow's, were fidgeting, twisting a large onyx ring.

"Seriously," said Strode, "I don't need some bastard who died when Queen Victoria was still a hottie ruining my business. So I'm here to cut a deal. You know the story, what will it take to get rid of the troublesome boy?"

"You believe in ghosts, now?" asked Mountford.

"I believe in money and power and death," Strode shot back. "I have the first two, Tommy has the third. I want to make it clear to him that his day is past, his haunting is pointless, his precious show can't go on. That's all."

Mountford shrugged.

"I'm impressed, in spite of myself," she admitted. "You're not quite the ignorant barbarian I assumed. But you need a medium for this, not a professor of history."

"You must know something!" insisted Strode. "At least give me a tip on where to start. I'll pay you for your trouble, if that's what you're worried about."

The academic pondered for a moment, then said, "According to all the stories, Tommy starts each haunting at the top of the thunder run, then goes down the ladder to die at the bottom, stage left."

"So if I could get to the silly bugger before he bashes his own head in, I might talk some sense into him?"

Strode felt a pang of doubt. But it was the best idea he had heard.

"Hoy, Gary, move your arse!" he shouted. "Which level would be at the same height as the roof of the Adelphi?"

Reluctantly, Marlow got out of the BMW, took out his tablet, and brought up old floor plans on screen.

"I reckon it would be the top level, boss," he said. "Most of this place is underground, so—"

"Yeah, yeah," interrupted Strode. "Right, let's get up there and I'll face the little sod down."

Marlow did not move.

"Get in the car, Gary!" growled Strode. "Or don't make any long term financial plans. Your choice."

Marlow moved closer to Mountford, looked down at his shoes.

"Right, bugger off then," shouted Strode, climbing into the sedan. "I'll deal with you later!"

It took him three minutes to spiral his way up the vast structure. As he hurled the car around corners and up ramps, he heard a rumbling sound above the protests of gears and brakes.

"Yeah, Tommy, you give it the works!" he said grimly. "We'll see who can make the most noise."

The thundering sound died out as he stopped the BMW in the middle of the top level and got out. Strode looked around, saw no signs of life, and walked around to the trunk.

"Well, Tommy Trouble," he said, "let's see how you cope with a bit of old-school magic."

A few months after the nightmares had begun, Strode had started Googling hauntings, ghosts, and exorcisms. He soon realized that his public image would be damaged by trying to involve a spiritualist, let alone the clergy. But he gleaned that less powerful spirits could be curbed by other means. He lifted a large plastic sack, one of several, out of the trunk and set off for the exit ramp. Strode felt watched, was sure eyes were focused on his back, but did not bother to look round. When he reached the top of the ramp, he opened the neck of the sack and began to pour its contents across the roadway.

"Ordinary sea-salt, Tommy," he said. "Said to be the ideal barrier to all occult forces. Let's give it a try. And if this doesn't work, well, I've got a few other tricks. Amazing what you can get online these days, isn't it? Oh, sorry, I forgot. You got killed before they had electricity, never mind computers."

After salting the exit ramp, Strode continued to lay a line of salt around the edge of the entire parking deck. He was half done when the rumbling began again, a steady vibration that circled him like a predator calculating its best line of attack.

"Do your worst, you little bastard!" he shouted, picking up his pace. "Got you rattled, eh?"

The source of the rumbling stopped moving, was now definitely coming from just ahead of Strode. The sound grew louder. Then the boy appeared, without any CGI preamble. One second the view was of fresh concrete and yellow-lined parking bays. Then Tommy was falling forward a couple of yards in front of the businessman, the boy's bloody brains spilling out onto the gray floor.

"Shit!"

Reeling back, Strode dropped the sack of salt, and it burst. Tommy vanished as suddenly as he had appeared, the splash of red and white matter gone as if it had never been.

"Cheap tricks!" bellowed Strode. "If that's the best you got, you got nothing!"

He set off back to the BMW, determined to finish the salt ring and then use some of the more advanced items he had obtained thanks to his wealth and tenacity. But as he turned on his heel the thundering noise returned, oddly changed. Something small and dully shining moved in the corner of his eye. Before he could focus on it, he felt a terrible impact in his ankle, heard bone crunch. Pain more intense than any he had felt before shot through his leg, and he pitched forward, landing heavily on his hands and knees.

A speckled iron cannonball rolled briskly past, just a few inches below his eyes. The metal sphere continued across the deck and then rolled out of sight down the exit ramp.

"You were warned, silly, fat man!"

The voice in his ear was gleeful, that of a child enjoying being naughty.

"You evil little prick!" cried Strode, weeping in pain. He struggled upright and started to hobble to the BMW. The sound of distant thunder returned, growing rapidly louder.

"No!" he moaned, casting anxious glances around the level. Again came the flicker of movement, but this time he was ready for it, tried to jump over the cannonball. He had forgotten his damaged ankle, and while his clumsy hop saved him from another hit, he landed badly. The pain was searing, now.

"Leave me alone!"

Memories of childhood bullying mingled with humiliations of adolescence and youth, a rogues' gallery of persecutors running through his head.

"You won't beat me! I always win!" he gasped, climbing into the BMW and slamming the door. He waited for another ball to appear, knowing one could damage the vehicle. Perhaps even immobilize it.

Don't get trapped up here! Moving target!

Strode started the engine and clashed the car into gear. The roar of German engineering made it impossible to hear the next ball, and it was moving swiftly and too low to see. But Strode felt it clearly enough as it smashed into the right rear wheel with a sickening metallic crunch. The car slewed, the damaged wheel screeching, and Strode struggled to avoid hitting the walls of the exit ramp.

"Not good enough, Tommy boy!" he said, regaining control. "Soon be out of here, then we can arrange a rematch."

He glanced at the rear view mirror, glad he had had the sense to close the trunk. At the top of the ramp, he glimpsed a brown-and-gray clad figure, its head mostly reddish mush, raising a hand.

"Wave me goodbye, eh?"

The throbbing pain in Strode's ankle made breaking difficult and the car kept picking up speed as he headed for the lower level and safety. He had to focus entirely on control, and so didn't hear the rumbling until the ball was almost upon him. He glimpsed a huge, curved shape in the wing mirror, a ball vastly larger than any old-time cannon could have fired.

It's the size of a bloody fridge! That's cheating, that's against the rules!

Strode swerved off the exit ramp onto an intermediate level, but not quite in time. The four-foot wide iron ball sideswiped the BMW, knocked it skidding crazily sideways. Strode felt the car lifting onto two wheels, prayed for it to stay upright. It did, but landed with a jarring crunch that again shot bolts of pain through his injured leg.

The engine cut. Strode began to pray aloud as he twisted at the ignition.

"Please God don't let it, please God don't let it—"

The car started just as a ball, at a good six feet across, appeared on the ramp from above. It thundered towards Strode as he screeched around in a handbrake turn, feeling the BMW's battered mechanism protest. Again, the ball sideswiped the car, spinning it wildly until it slammed into the concrete wall. Strode, who had not had time to buckle up, struck his head against the doorjamb and blacked out.

***

"Did you hear that?"

Isadora Mountford paused in the act of climbing into her Fiat, cocked an ear.

"Sounds like thunder," she said. "Would you like a lift? Or are you going to wait here for your boss?"

Marlow stood, the picture of indecision.

"You really care about that ghastly man, don't you?" asked the woman. "Amazing."

"I should have gone with him," said Marlow. "Can you take me up?"

It was Mountford's turn to hesitate. The rumbling noise grew, then died away.

"All right, get in," she said.

As they ascended the car park they made awkward introductions, and Marlow asked if Tommy had ever seriously injured anyone.

"No," said Mountford. "But remember he was previously bound to the Adelphi. Part of the building's fabric, really. Who knows what he might be able to do if freed from what one might call his original contract of employment."

"You mean he might be like asbestos?" asked Marlow. "Better left alone."

"Or got rid of by real experts, yes," said the woman, smiling. "Though your analogy is a tad prosaic for my—"

She stopped as the Fiat reached the third level, halfway to the top.

"Christ Almighty!" exclaimed Marlow.

The concrete roadway was badly cracked, as if a huge juggernaut or maybe a tank had passed this way.

"I know the specifications of that stuff," said Marlow quietly, as Mountford drove them off the ramp. "Nothing that could drive in through the entrance would be heavy enough to break it."

"And yet broken it is."

Mountford stopped and got out, Marlow following cautiously.

"Look," he said, pointing to skid marks on the cracked floor. "Boss came in here, in a hurry."

"Then where is he?" demanded the academic.

They looked around in puzzlement, seeing no sign of the silver BMW. Then Marlow pointed at the far corner of the parking space.

"Just a few bits of junk," opined Mountford, as they walked over.

"I can't see how this is relevant—"

Again, she stopped talking and stood, staring in puzzlement at the patch of debris. Now she was a bit closer there was something familiar about it. The silver color, for one thing. Fragments of tinted glass lay in a spray pattern around a roughly rectangular object. There were also patches of a red so dark it was almost black under the strip lights.

"Oh Jesus, oh God," exclaimed Marlow. "What has he done?"

"Good question," said Mountford, "let's go."

They hurried back to the Fiat. Mountford was just driving onto the bottom level when they heard the thunder again, and the square patch of daylight at the exit was blocked by a great, round shape.

* * *

Faces
By A.I. Nasser

"Dr. Riley!"

The voice was old, raspy, almost inaudible if not for the fact that I was listening for it. I turned, as did the six or seven other gentlemen standing in a semi-circle around me, listening to my newest surgical conquests. I smiled at the man striding across the large foyer towards me. He held a cigar in one hand, and the slender arm of a beautiful brunette in the other, both smiling, but only one of them genuinely.

The older man didn't seem all too pleased to see me.

"Dr. Alcott," I greeted, giving a slight bow, briefly acknowledging the young woman with a gentle smile. "It's been too long."

"Indeed, it has been," Alcott replied. He kept his gaze fixed on me, an alarmingly challenging look if I did not know better. "I'm quite surprised that you were able to make it to my gathering, what with your busy schedule and all."

I raised my glass in a silent toast and winked at him. "I could not imagine missing it, Dr. Alcott," I said. "A man of your stature deserves to be celebrated for all his achievements. What would it say about me if I were not to make an appearance at such a gracious event?"

"Quite a lot, I would imagine," Alcott chuckled, although his eyes reflected a darker sentiment.

I turned my attention to the young woman, took her hand and kissed it. "And may I assume that this fine young woman is your daughter?"

"Your flattery is almost suffocating, Dr. Riley," Alcott laughed, gazing hard at the others in a silent order that they laugh along with him.

They did.

"Anna," the young woman introduced herself. "Granddaughter."

I feigned surprise. "Dr. Alcott, you will forgive me," I said, "but it was quite miraculous that even as a grandfather, you still make the rest of us seem so small. I applaud you, sir, and feel humbled in your presence."

"Enough of that, Riley," Alcott smiled, attempting to hide the annoyance in his voice. He chuckled, eyeing the rest of the group, faking an attitude of control I could easily see through. It wasn't a surprise that he would be uneasy with me being here. We were, after all, rivals, and although he had come to speak of me as simply 'that other doctor', I had heard the whispers. He detested my existence in this world, in his sphere of influence. I was a threat to everything that made him unique. I was the younger version of him, the man who would eventually surpass him and make his accomplishments seem trivial.

I did little to hide the fact that I understood this, and even as I sipped from my glass, I kept my eyes locked on his. There was fury there. A fire. Hatred, even. I relished every moment of it.

"Well, you must excuse me, gentlemen," he said to the men standing around me, purposely ignoring me. "I have other guests to greet and see to. I leave you in the capable hands of Dr. Riley." He looked at me. "Try not to bore them with the dreams of young minds that have yet much to learn."

"I would never imagine it," I smiled, raising my glass again. "A toast, to Dr. Alcott and his achievements." I gave Anna a quick wink, one I was sure Alcott noticed. "Each and every one of them."

Anna smiled at me, and was hastily pulled away. She glanced back at me over her shoulder, a quick gesture that could be mistaken for a flick of hair.

I knew better, of course. I would be seeing Anna again very soon.

***

The chill night air had found its way into my coat, and despite the warmth my clothes had promised to provide, I found myself shivering against the cool wind. The streets were devoid of any kind of life, save for the random rat here and there, scurrying from its hiding place to sniff at horse manure that decorated the cobbled streets of London. The light from the gas lamps flickered, casting long shadows against the dirty bricks of the buildings around me. Behind closed shutters, the soft voices of those who were still awake seemed to seep out, hushed whispers that found a way to coil around me and tickle my ears.

I loved the night. I felt at home here, in the quiet darkness that was only ever disturbed by the sound of my walking and the occasional burst of laughter from a dark alleyway. The streets of London had a way of encompassing me, drawing me into their embrace with their filth and mysteries, a stark contrast to the bright and shining life of the elite dinner parties and gatherings I had grown to hate.

The streets. This is where I thrived. This is where I felt the most at home. Like a character out of R. L. Stevenson's *Jekyll and Hyde*, I was enthralled by what the darkness promised.

The sound of wheels on cobblestones and the faint ring of a bell made me turn around. Through the growing fog and the shadows, a carriage made its way towards me, lazy and awkward like a toddler that had just learned to stand on its own two feet. It stopped beside me, and a door opened, showering me in a bright light that made me cringe. The disturbance was annoying, except for the lovely face that was smiling down at me when my eyes finally adjusted and I could see Anna Alcott clearly.

"It would be shameful of me to leave you to walk home, Dr. Riley," the beautiful brunette said, her eyes glowing and her smile warm. "Please, do come in."

I tipped my hat and climbed into the carriage. As soon as I had settled into the seat opposite her, the door securely fastened behind me, the carriage lurched and continued on its way.

"A somber night to be walking the streets of London, wouldn't you agree, doctor?" Anna asked.

"The night is a friend," I replied. "As doctors, we work hard to understand the unknown, and what is more mysterious than the dark?"

Anna smiled, her hands folded on her lap. "I can see why my grandfather hates you," she said.

"The cockiness, I presume?"

"The confidence," she countered.

I smiled. "Your grandfather is not very fond of varying opinions," I said, "and that is all I can say on the matter."

"Oh, I believe you have much more to say," Anna laughed, a soft giggle that would have been mistaken for child-like if I had not been gazing directly at the source. "If you are in no great hurry, I would be most honored if you would join me at our home for a cup of tea and some friendly conversation."

"What would Dr. Alcott think?"

Anna's smile widened, a bit mischievously. "Dr. Alcott does not need to know."

I returned the smile, and we continued the rest of the journey in silence.

***

The Alcott residence was quite magnificent, its splendor made even more impressive by the wide grounds around it. It was almost as if it occupied an alcove of magic in the midst of an otherwise gloomy city. Anna escorted me into the house, and gave me a quick tour of the main living area before leading me to the library. The room was stacked with books from wall to wall, and on one side, a large fireplace took residence, like a king on his throne. Around the fireplace were a pair of Untermyer armchairs, and Anna gently gestured to one.

"This is quite impressive," I commented, squinting in the candlelight as I tried to make out the titles of some of the books nearest to me.

"My grandfather loves his antiques," Anna said as she rang a bell on the center table.

The butler that came in was a gigantic, looming figure. His face was half-hidden by the shadows, but I could still make out the misshapen structure of his jaw, and the grotesque way one eye seemed to hang lower than the other, as if sagging under some unseen weight. He stared at me for a second longer than what would have been considered polite, and I felt my body shudder under his gaze.

"Tea, Walter, if you please," Anna said.

The man only grunted, looked at me once more, and slowly trudged out of the library. I watched him leave.

"He's quite harmless," Anna assured me, as if reading my mind.

"I would doubt that very much," I replied.

"So, tell me, doctor, what brings you to London?"

I relaxed, letting the fire warm my bones from the night chill that had found their way to them, and from the lingering image of Walter.

"Medicine, of course," I replied.

"Oh, I understand that," Anna said, her eyes fixated on mine. There was a confidence there that greatly mirrored that of her grandfather's. "I merely ask why?"

"What better place to continue your career than in London?" I smiled. "The opportunities are vast, the possibilities endless. A man can grow quickly and successfully here. Your grandfather can attest to that."

"I'm sure," Anna nodded, turning to stare into the flames. The logs cackled, firing small sparks that quickly disappeared. "My grandfather has made himself quite a fortune since coming to this city."

I frowned. "You are not a London native?"

Anna turned back to me and smiled. "Of course," she said. "I am. My grandfather, on the other hand, is from Edinburgh. Although you would not have guessed it."

My eyes widened. "I would not," I agreed. "There is not a hint of a Scottish accent in his voice."

"He's a chameleon of sorts," Anna nodded. "Changes faces faster than anyone I know. He has always taught me that to survive in this world, one must have a dynamic personality, an eagerness to bend with the tides."

"Sound advice."

"And I would do well to heed it," Anna said, looking back to the flames. "It seems, with the way the world is changing, it is advice that must not be ignored."

"Indeed," I agreed.

The sound of cups clattering against saucers interrupted the silence we had fallen into, and I did my best not to turn and watch Walter enter the room. He worked silently for a man of his size, and I did my best to keep my eyes downcast. Nevertheless, I could feel him watching me, his gaze like a boulder on my chest. He handed me my cup, for which I thanked him, quickly and quietly, and he replied with a grunt.

After he left, I raised my eyes and met Anna's.

"Does he disturb you?" she asked.

"Not in the slightest," I lied, and I could see she didn't believe me. "To be frank, I question the reasoning behind his disfigurement."

"Do you mean what happened to him?"

"I would rather not intrude," I said, raising a hand to stop her. "A man's business is his own. Something *my* grandfather taught me. However, it does seem peculiar that, being in Dr. Alcott's employment, your grandfather would not have tried to remedy the man's predicament."

"And why would you call it a predicament?"

"What else should I call it?"

Anna smiled and took a sip of tea. "You see, I believe that is the true problem with surgeons," she said. "That you see everything as a medical issue that must be cut and resolved. You regard Walter as an anomaly, and immediately presume that he must be *fixed*. However, Dr. Riley, Walter does not need fixing. He is quite unique the way he is."

"I apologize," I said, taking a sip of my own tea and placing it on the table beside me. "I did not mean to be presumptuous."

"That is quite alright," Anna assured. "Walter has been in this family for years, generations even. My grandfather couldn't leave him behind in Edinburgh and brought him to London with him."

I frowned again. "He does not look old," I commented.

"How would you know?" Anna smiled. "You haven't properly looked at him."

I nodded and took another sip of my tea.

She was right, of course.

***

I woke up with a start.

The darkness engulfed me, surrounded me from all corners,

deep and overbearing that I could see nothing at all. It was almost as if I hadn't opened my eyes at all. I could not remember when I had dozed off, and a sudden rush of embarrassment hit me at the thought of having had fallen asleep in Anna's company.

But where was I?

I was no longer in the library, of that I was sure. For starters, I was lying down on my back, no longer propped up comfortably in my armchair with a cup of tea in my hands. The air was colder here, thicker, a lot more suffocating. There was no residual warmth coming from the fireplace, and the sheer lack of light, the darkness that was so complete, made it frighteningly clear that I was so far away from any light source worth mentioning.

My first instinct was that I had been brought up to a room, and I briefly shuddered at the thought of Walter carrying me like a baby, away from the library, away from the warmth. But even if this were a guest room of sorts, a candle would have been left for me. There was no reasonable explanation for someone to have left me in this darkness, a stranger in a strange place, with no bearings whatsoever.

I tried to move, but my limbs were heavy, and I merely rolled onto my side before falling in a heap from whatever bed I had been laid upon. I felt drowsy, my mind spinning and my eyes watering, and the cold stone floor cut through my skin and to my bones like knives of pure ice. It was then I realized that whoever had brought me here, had also stripped me of my clothes, and that I was naked, completely. I pushed myself to my knees and turned my head left and right, waiting for my eyes to adjust, as they should, to the dark. When that didn't happen, I fought back the panic and began to crawl across the stone floor.

I came across a wall, headfirst, feeling a sharp pain erupt at my forehead and quickly find its way down to my neck and spine. I let out an anguished hiss, and propped myself against the wall, ignoring the cold for the few seconds it took for the pain to subside. When it finally had, I tried to make sense of my situation.

If there is a wall, then there must eventually be a door.

The thought rippled through my mind, and I slowly pushed myself up to my feet. I patted the cold stones, moving slowly to one side in hopes of maybe finding a way out. The cold seeped up through my feet, numbing my toes and making each step feel like a toiled effort. I do not know how long I continued in this fashion, but I gasped in delight when my hands finally fell on a wooden frame, and soon enough, a handle.

I turned it, quickly, pushing the door open as I stumbled and fell into a long hall.

The lights blinded me, despite their dimness, and I shielded my eyes as I waited for my vision to adjust. The hallway was empty, devoid of any sort of furnishing that would give some clue as to where I was. This, in itself, frightened me. The torch above my head crackled as I took in my surroundings. It looked like I was in a catacombs of sort, below the house maybe, the hallway curving around a corner and blinding me from anything beyond.

My head spun, and I felt my stomach turn. I pushed myself onto my hands and knees, and tried to steady my breathing. The dampness was overpowering, and the cold air made my lungs scream in protest. My heartbeat quickened until I could feel my chest threatening to burst.

The tea.

Of course, it was the tea. This was a trap. Had always been one. Anna had not been enthralled by me. She had not wished to bring me here for what I had assumed would be a long night of gentle lovemaking. No. She had drugged me. Or Walter had. This was all a ruse. Alcott's hatred for me multiplied to a point where he would rather have me hidden away than admit to his defeat.

I needed to escape. If only my head would stop spinning and I could think clearer.

The sound of footsteps echoed in the hallway, and a sudden burst of adrenaline brought me to my feet. I tried to discern the direction from which the sound was coming from, and when I could not, decided to choose a direction at random and follow it.

My feet slapped silently against the cold stone floor as I moved. I closed my mouth, trying to force my breaths through my nose, fearing that any sound I made would give me away. The footsteps grew quieter until they finally stopped. I paused in my escape. Frowning. Concentrating. Listening for any sound that could give me a clue as to what I was to expect.

The footsteps returned suddenly, this time quicker, running. Whoever was back there, they had found out that I was no longer in the room. They were coming for me.

I threw caution to the wind and ran. The hallway twisted and turned, and in the dim light of the hanging torches, I gasped for breath as I pushed myself forward. The running grew louder, my pursuer closing in on me, and my heart jumped in my chest when I heard a distant grunt echo down the narrow passage to my ear. I was suddenly very aware of who or what was chasing me, and the thought of seeing that grotesque face come for me in the dark pushed me to run even faster.

I ran like a man possessed, my muscles screaming with the strain I was putting them under. Strain they were not accustomed to. And the echoing sound of Walter's pursuit only grew louder. I turned around, saw nothing in the shadows cast by the torches, and pushed harder. I needed to escape. I could not imagine what that monster would do to me once I was in its clutches once more.

I turned a corner and screamed in triumph at the sight of a cell door, and beyond that, stairs. I almost jumped the remaining distance to it, all too aware that Walter was closing in on me quickly. I pushed the door open, throwing my weight against it, and felt it slam back into me and send me flying back. I hit the ground hard, my head spinning even more, and quickly pushed to my feet. The door had ricocheted off the bottom stair, for it had been meant to be pulled, not pushed, and I had been too foolish to notice in my haste.

I jumped onto my feet and raced forward, determined to make my escape, when a large hand wrapped around my neck and pulled me back, screaming.

***

"You must bend with the tides."

The voice came from far away.

I opened my eyes, slowly, immediately welcomed by a pulsating pain in the back of my head. I was lying on my back again, and as my vision began to clear, the haze on my eyes slowly disappearing, I turned my head towards the voice.

Anna sat in a chair beside me, her hands folded neatly on her lap, her hair flowing in waves down her shoulders. I tried to get up, but I could not move, the sounds of chains rattling and the cold feel of steel cutting into my skin. I turned away from the woman sitting beside me, and noticed the shackles around my hands and feet. I fought against the restraints, but I was held down fast, unable to move. I was trapped. Obviously, Anna would not make the same mistake twice.

"You were not supposed to wake up so quickly," she said, making me turn back to face her.

"What are you doing?" I shouted. "Undo these shackles immediately."

Anna laughed, no longer the child-like giggle from before, but a much more sinister cackle. It echoed off the walls and pierced my ears, sending shivers down my spine.

"My dear doctor," Anna cooed. "You are in no position to make demands. Actually, you are in no position to do anything at all."

"Did your grandfather plan all this?" I demanded. "Did he ask you to bring me here? To drug me and then subdue me in this manner?"

Anna tilted her head to one side, the smile never leaving her face, and looked at me in pity. "You are such a spectacular specimen, Dr. Riley," she finally said.

"A specimen?" I frowned at her. "What in heaven's name are you talking about?"

She chuckled and looked past me. I turned and followed her gaze, feeling myself shrink as Walter materialized from the shadows, his looming figure towering over me like the angel of death had come to collect me. In the light, his deformities stood out even more. His nose was crooked, as if he had broken it multiple times and had never had it heal properly. His eyes were as dark as obsidians, one much lower than the other, far lower than I had previously observed. His jaw also seemed to sag, and hung at an obscure, almost impossible angle. The skin on his cheeks looked like ripples of water, as if he were wearing a mask that didn't quite fit.

He looked at me and smiled, and I felt a part of my soul shatter into pieces and disappear into an abyss of nothingness as I stared in horror at his visage.

"Unique, is he not?" Anna asked.

Her voice was no longer enchanting. No longer reassuring, gentle, welcoming, calm. It was laced with a manic sort of glee at my discomfort, and an undertone of bitterness.

"Let me go," I pleaded. "Let me go, and I will never speak of this to anyone."

"I have complete faith that you will not."

"I will leave," I quickly added. "I will disappear. I will take all my belongings ... no, I will not even do that. I will just go. Leave London. Never again be a threat to your grandfather."

"Oh, do be quiet," Anna said, waving a hand, exasperated and frustrated now that I had stooped so low as to beg. "James Alcott is not my grandfather. That would be quite distasteful if it were true."

"It does not matter," I stammered. "I do not care who or what he is to you. I will leave him be. I will take my medicine and find some corner of the world where he will never have to hear from me again. India! Yes, India! I will leave for India immediately!"

"That would be a shame," Anna replied. "He is quite fond of you. I remember him saying that you remind him of a younger version of himself." She paused, her eyes boring into mine. "A version he would most like to live again."

I opened my mouth in an attempt to try a different approach to win my freedom, but all that came out was a pathetic whimper and a gasp for air. I was shaking, the cold and fear taking over, making the shackles around my wrists and ankles clang. Anna smiled at me, a cold curl of the lips I knew spelt nothing good for me.

Anna stood up, slowly crossed the short distance to where I lay, and looked down at me. "Men of science have always been narrow minded," he said. "You believe yourselves to be Gods on this earth, when in reality, you are oblivious to the mysteries of it all. Of what hides in the shadows. Of the beings that live right beside you, that you are too blind to notice. You comprehend little of this world, Dr. Riley. Such an unfortunate waste of the mind."

The door behind her opened before I could reply, and she turned to look at her guest. "James!" she greeted. "We have been waiting for you."

I tried to shift positions, an attempt to strain my neck and look beyond the curvaceous figure of the woman as she blocked the view of the door. There was a slight chuckle, a shuffling of feet, and soft footsteps that seemed to come from everywhere. James Alcott stepped into view, and I immediately fell back, hoping that the table I was tied to would somehow open and hide me within its structure.

The eyes.

It was the eyes that scared me the most. There was a menacing hunger there, a deep hatred mixed with a slight satisfaction that only a predator would save for its prey. They blazed with a desire to hurt me, to tear me apart from limb to limb, to make me suffer unspeakable pain. All of this I saw in his eyes, and in the slow curl of the man's lips as a smile materialized below them.

"My dear, Dr. Riley," James Alcott snarled. "I do hope you are utterly uncomfortable."

"Dr. Alcott, please," I begged. "I beseech you, let me go. I have told your granddaughter that I would sooner disappear than seek any form of retribution here. I will leave this wretched city and its inhabitants, and you will never see me again."

"Ludicrous," Dr. Alcott chuckled. "Heavens no, I could not imagine this city without a Dr. Riley. You have so much to give, so much to achieve. I would not deprive London of the miracles Dr. Riley will one day perform."

His words were like daggers, the mocking tone making my skin crawl. A harsh grunt brought my head around to Walter as he pushed a tray of surgical tools by my side, and then looked up to James Alcott with a grotesque smile that looked completely unnatural.

"Ah, Walter," Alcott nodded. "Always in a hurry."

"What are you doing?"

Alcott shifted his gaze towards me, leaned against the table, and pursed his lips, as if readying himself for a long lecture. He seemed fatigued, beyond the stress of just having had attended a party in his honor. It was more a wearing of time, as if the universe had hacked away at him for far too long, and age was slowly becoming the nightmarish obstacle that could no longer be crossed.

"Time is not our friend, wouldn't you agree, Dr. Riley?"

I tried to reply, but the massive hand that suddenly rested on my chest, crushing the breath from my lungs, made that impossible.

"You see, to truly achieve greatness, one needs time," Alcott explained, nodding to Anna who disappeared from view. "Unfortunately, time is not a commodity one can easily replace. This second is not like the last, nor in any way similar to the one that will come. But to live forever?" Alcott raised a finger and shook it slowly at me. "Now that is truly a miracle."

I shook my head, unable to comprehend what the man was trying to tell me. I tried to shift my position, but Walter's hand on my chest kept me paralyzed in place. I looked at the butler, and he smiled back at me. For a brief second, I felt like the skin around his mouth had broken.

No. Slipped.

That was the word.

The skin sagged and revealed his gums, as if it had been held in place by some form of stitching, and was now loose once more. I watched in horror as more of the skin around his chin folded upon itself, and the glistening of underlying muscle slowly showed itself. Walter noticed what I was staring at, and quickly receded, hiding in the shadows and fiddling with his face.

I turned to Alcott, my eyes wide, and gasped something incoherent now that the weight on my chest was gone. Alcott was watching Walter with pity, then turned back to me.

"However, no miracle is true, and immortality comes at a price," he said, shaking his head. "Is that not the case, my dear Anna?"

Anna stepped back into view and smiled at James. He folded her into his arms, gave her a long and passionate kiss, and then took the scalpel she had ready for him.

"She is your granddaughter," I stammered, although the real horror was in the way he looked down at me with the scalpel in his hand.

"She is my wife," Alcott corrected. "For centuries, she has been nothing less, and always more." He looked at her and smiled. "It took me quite a few killings before we finally found a face she liked."

"Killings?" I choked.

Alcott chuckled and gently grabbed my chin, turning my head from side to side, inspecting me. "Yes, well, East London is filled with prostitutes no one will ever truly miss. And you, Dr. Riley, have a face that has already garnered a respectable following."

Before I could reply, Walter's hand fell back down upon my chest, and Alcott leaned in over me. "A fine face, indeed," he whispered.

My screams filled the room as the cold steel began slicing across my jaw.

***

London Daily Post, October 10th, 1889
Renowned surgeon dies at 65

The London medical community was shocked at the news of Doctor James Anthony Alcott's death last night. Dr. Alcott was discovered in his London residence by granddaughter Anna William Alcott, his only surviving relative and heir to the Alcott fortune. The great doctor was known for his groundbreaking achievements in the surgical field, and will be forever remembered as an innovator and practitioner of remarkable talent. Dr. John Riley said it best during the memorial service, that Dr. Alcott was 'a great man who will forever be remembered, and greatly missed, by all who respected his work.'

***

London Daily Post, September 7th, 1890
Alcott heiress weds surgical wunderkind

Anna William Alcott and Doctor John Fitzgerald Riley were married on September 4th, 1890. The wedding announcement comes almost a year after the death of Dr. James Alcott, surprising many who had watched the rivalry between Anna Alcott's grandfather and her new husband. Speculations have risen regarding Dr. Riley's desire for a share of the Alcott fortune, which Anna Alcott has inherited as the sole living relative of the late Dr. James Alcott. However, close friends of the heiress assure that these are just rumors.

* * *

Initial Impression
By David Longhorn

Editor's Note: The following story was found among the effects of the late John Atkinson Grimwade, arguably the most successful British horror writer of our time. As with all of the author's works, it had been written in longhand. It was then prepared as a formal manuscript on an Imperial manual typewriter, the same machine upon which Grimwade wrote all his classic novels and short fiction.

Along with the typescript, I found a note from my lifelong friend and client instructing me to make this story available on the internet at the stroke of midnight (GMT), October 31st. I confess that, at the time, I was struck by the peculiarity of the request. Grimwade had always expressed utter contempt for all things digital—hence his reliance on antiquated technology in the production of his novels and short stories. For him to insist that his last work should be freely available as an 'electronic download' struck me as bizarre.

But of course, at the time, I was preoccupied with more urgent matters. I had gone to Grimwade's apartment in the pleasant heart of Canterbury, anticipating business as usual. For nearly forty years, I had been visiting Grimwade at progressively more salubrious addresses, seeking to winkle out of him his latest tour de force. My old friend would have been the first to admit that he was not always an easy client.

I could never be sure what he would have for me. Would it be a finely-crafted tale of supernatural horror, such as Venus with Six Fingers or The Bloody Glass? Or might it be another of the paperback 'pot-boilers' my friend churned out under a bewildering array of pen-names (Frank Trencherman, Royce Rollison, Lee Grant to name but three) throughout his career? Grimwade affected to despise the pulp fiction that paid his bills. And what literary man could be proud of novels like *Gloria's Gory Go-Go Girls*, *The Brainripper Chronicles*, or *A Fistful of Gonads*? Yet he always talked over their plots and key incidents with a certain lip-smacking relish.

As the world now knows, what I found was my friend's body, his hand still clutching the fateful glass that he had drained of poison. And on his Regency credenza lay the story you are about to read. My initial impression was that it is not especially good, and I have to admit that it has not grown upon me to any discernible degree. However, a friend's last request should be honored.

I am sure some will make a great deal of the fact that I am mentioned directly in this tale. It was typical of Grimwade to make jokes at my expense, and I am sure many fans are already aware that I appear—usually quite thinly disguised—in several of his books. I am eviscerated in *High Jinks at Slasham Hall*, gradually dismembered in *Choppy Go Lucky*, and unceremoniously pushed into a rotary cultivator by the eponymous anti-hero of *Nasty Nick*. I never took these fictional assassinations seriously, and reports that they always followed disputes over advances have been greatly exaggerated.

I feel sure that other, more discerning critics, will see that the author's insistence that his last work of fiction is in fact nothing of the sort, and falls into a hallowed literary tradition. To blur the distinction between artifice and reality is hardly new. Enjoy the story for what it is, gentle reader; a flight of fancy by a remarkable author who, for reasons still unclear, decreed that it must be his swan song.

Aubrey Jolyon, Senior Editor, Gorelock Books

***

Very nervous? Yes, of course. But that is only natural. I am embarking upon a perilous voyage. I am going to that 'borne from which no traveler returns', as the Bard puts it. Very overrated, Shakespeare, in my opinion. But one can't say such things when one is alive. Odd that imminent death should feel so liberating. But I digress.

Every great venture begins with a sacrifice. In this case the sacrifice is not my mortal coil, which that gormless clown Jolyon will discover in an hour or so after I finish typing this. I only hope he doesn't drop dead from shock on the spot. He is so *very* unhealthy, with his great fat belly and boozer's nose. But even if he does perish, this manuscript will be found and someone will do what is necessary.

Now, to get back to my point; it is not my body that I am giving up in a bargain with the greatest 'closer' of all. It is, as more astute readers will have already guessed, my immortal soul that I have signed away. And that is why I am writing this story which is not a story; it is a work of fact disguised as fiction.

Intrigued? Gentle reader, soon you will be amazed. And then appalled, and quite probably terrified. But only for a little while...

The unusual journey I have taken began with a vague disgust for life that slowly grew to embrace everything. For years now, I have found writing detailed descriptions of protracted suffering and violent death extremely cathartic. It's not just fat, old Jolyon I kill over and over again. My idiot relatives, my cretinous neighbors, the low-life scum whose drunken carousing outside the Green Man interrupts my work, leisure time, or sleep—all perish, again and again, in my stories.

Silly? Perhaps. But then we are very silly little creatures, we humans. Some of us fondly style ourselves 'Masters of the Universe', while most put faith in some caring deity or other. But I have become convinced that, while there is a god of sorts, He, She, or It has long since absconded from this realm. We have been left to the not-very-tender mercies of a rather different order of being.

"Ah, but that's just old-fashioned cynicism—an easy pose to strike for a rich man like you." True, I have always been something of a cynic. I could not churn out a steady stream of drivel about psychopaths and Satanists if I were not. But anyone who has read my best work closely will know that I am a little more thoughtful than the dimwits who devour my garish bestsellers.

To be honest, I have no respect whatsoever for my audience. They're even stupider than Jolyon, by and large. Isn't that deliciously shocking? But seriously, anyone who wants to spend their time reading trash like *Citadel of Putrefaction* must be a congenital imbecile, or at most only slightly higher on the evolutionary scale. As for the pimply, pubescent morons who flocked to see clumsy, low-budget film adaptations of my pot-boilers—trash such as *Zombie Bikers Must Die* or *Kiss the Blood off My Chainsaw*—well, once I would have despaired for the future of civilization. Once.

A writer is a slave to his readership, after all, and yet he is at the same time a tyrant. He commands them to read his words, drink deep of the wine of his imagination. And they do! Yet, if he makes a single misstep, he risks breaking the spell. Then he becomes unfashionable, his books are remaindered, and people start asking, "Is old 'What's-his-name' still writing, then? I thought he'd died years ago."

No, for all that it offers the odd flicker of satisfaction, a writer's life is at best precarious and at worst miserable. If you are foolish enough to socialize, people find out what you do and generally come up with either of two responses. One is to ask you 'where you get your ideas'. The other is to offer you a 'sure fire bestseller, guaranteed smash hit, so all you have to do is write it'. And they generously undertake to split the proceeds fifty-fifty, of course. I stopped going to parties a long time ago.

Again, though, I digress. Humor an old man! And a condemned man at that. Condemned by myself, it is true, but still. On the one hand, the imminent transition to another state of being is exhilarating, but on the other it does make one a trifle giddy. Focus, Johnny. Get it done. What looms is, after all, your last and greatest deadline!

So, what am I playing at? Why this rambling account of my state of mind just before I 'throw a seven', to coin a barbarous phrase? What could prompt a man of wealth, a middle-ranking celebrity, an author who has yet to lose his mass appeal, to commit self-murder? A man who might well, in fact, have lived to a hundred in comfort?

"Perhaps the balance of his mind is disturbed?" Hmm. Writers do tend to go a bit barmy in their declining years, I agree. Many sink into drink-sodden decrepitude, brains decaying along with their livers. But, as Jolyon can attest, I have never over-indulged in alcohol or any other stimulant.

Equally easy to blame is sex, of course. Or rather, the lack of it. I would not be the first man in late middle-age to sink into a depression over declining potency. But I had my fair share of erotic encounters in my younger days. So many adorable young things at conventions willing to drop in on me at my suite, usually bringing a bottle, invariably offering their bodies to some extent. No, I have my memories. Having amassed a fortune in fleshly joy, I could live on the interest for many years more.

"Sex, alcohol, drugs—does nothing else interest this man?" I have already stated my disgust for my own species, at this shoddy Barnum and Bailey world I am forced to inhabit. In my books I exact extravagant revenge on individuals, groups, and mankind in general. But some ten years ago, an idea, absurd on the face of it, popped into my head. Or, more likely, was put there...

The notion that I might call upon the dark forces I had so often been forced to imagine was the tiny grain of sand in the oyster of my imagination. Around it formed a very dark and lustrous pearl—a jewel fit for the Prince of Darkness himself, in fact.

It was very simple. I had spent many years researching all things arcane and occult so as to make my books seem authentic. Of course, I had faked and fudged all over the place, changing genuine spells and curses to better fit my plots. At first I had felt a kind of jovial contempt for people who really believed such stuff—Satanists, Wiccans and the like. Then one night I woke, perhaps during the witching hour itself, with the realization that I was now equipped to be a genuine sorcerer. *But could any of it really work?*

First, I attempted a few simple curses. The raucous drunks spilling out of the pub opposite my flat were permanently silenced when a night bus ploughed into them as they waited to cross the street. The bus driver later swore that a 'thing with a horrible face' startled him, causing him to lose control of the vehicle. Of course, CCTV footage showed nothing of the kind. The poor man lost his job, sad to say. But he was the first of many pawn sacrifices in a long game, as I tested the limits of my powers.

Eventually I grew bored. Yes, I had eliminated a few troublesome individuals. There was the spiteful reviewer who kept sneering at my work; a couple of younger authors who had threatened to eclipse me; a politician whose approach to personal taxation offended me. But then I came to realize that in killing off a few individuals I was really just whiling away my declining years. And, after all, is murder such a great achievement? A mindless virus or a loose roof slate that can kill a man. Even the knowledge that I would never be caught no longer thrilled me.

Resolved to achieve something of more lasting value, I returned to my extensive library of occult tomes. I looked more closely at rituals designed to extend one's lifespan and power over the world. It was tempting to think of myself as an immortal tyrant, ruling over a cowed humanity. But even that vision started to pall. Because, in the final analysis, people would still be idiots. One might as well aspire to be emperor of an ant farm. No, better to destroy this pathetic human world, especially if in doing so one could become a superior being.

Monstrous? Perhaps I am. But, as I have already remarked, there is something exhilarating about one's imminent demise. After extensive research and some preliminary negotiations, I am convinced that I have found a copper-bottomed way of ending pestiferous mankind.

Unless I am very much mistaken, the way in which I can become a god is to bring about the Apocalypse. It seems that Lucifer, for all his power, cannot directly intervene in human affairs without a gilt-edged invitation from a mortal.

No, don't stop reading. Whatever you do, continue to the end. After all, you want to find out what happens, don't you? Though of course if you are reading this, you will already know a little.

Do you know how to bring about the end of the world? One must simply invite the former Archangel Lucifer to do his worst—or should that be his best? 'Come, Satan, Destroyer of Worlds!' That, in essence, is the invocation that I am required to make, though not in English. Odd, but there it is. Latin, it seems, is still the official language of Hell. But of course, it is not quite so simple. Otherwise any ranting, half-wit, could bring about Armageddon whenever he stubbed his toe. No, the very precise terms of my contract with the cloven-footed gentleman state that the Latin version of the invocation must be propagated throughout the world in the course of a single day—All Hallows' Eve. What's more, the fatal phrase must be planted in the minds of readers without them realizing that they are being primed for destruction.

Impossible, you say? Once I would have agreed with you. But after I have typed the last line of this most contrived of true stories I will ingest the tincture without a qualm. I am sure that, sooner or later, the invocation will take effect. Perhaps it will come like a single, great lightning bolt. Or, more likely, it will take the form of terminal decay, the final triumph of invincible chaos over this fallen world. The Son of the Morning has not vouchsafed his plans to me in detail. But he strikes me as a very efficient operator, in his way. My only regret is that I never used him properly in any of my books.

***

Editor's Afterword: I feel I ought to spell out, to avoid any possible misunderstanding, that the above story is an elaborate joke, an exercise in black humor. It is written in the form of an acrostic, whereby the first letter of each paragraph spells out the supposed invocation Grimwade mentions. To save the reader further trouble the result is:

VENIT SATANAS PESTIFER MUNDI

It is of course absurd to suggest that such a clichéd and somewhat silly display of diabolism could have any effect, even if it had somehow burrowed into millions of readers' minds without their knowing on Halloween. But I must admit that it is a rather clever idea; that publishing such a story on the internet could bring about the end of the world. But please, do not judge my poor friend too harshly, you who are reading this story days, weeks, or even years after its appearance.

***

Your world is still perfectly intact, is it not?

* * *

Closer
By Sara Clancy

A dark figure lurked in the corner of her eyes, like something pressed upon the world instead of a part of it. A stain that marred the depths of the crowd that shoved in around her. Resolutely, she kept her eyes fixed forward, refusing to turn towards the figure. Having taken the same path home every workday for years, she knew the rules of train etiquette well. Keep your eyes forward, mind your own business, and move the second the doors open. So instead, she inched away as far as she could, using the people around her as a shield.

The train lurched as it slowed. Her tight grip on the safety rail was the only thing that kept her from being drowned in the flood of bodies squishing in around her, each jostling for position. She used the movement to sneak a glance over her shoulder but couldn't catch sight of the black mass again.

The scent of stale sweat and other things she didn't want to name filled her nose as she anxiously waited. She had managed to ignore it for most of the trip but now, with the platform edging closer at an agonizingly slow pace, the rank, humid air made her stomach cramp. It was impossible to keep from touching the other passengers, especially as they inched ever closer to the doors in restless anticipation. Cheap clothing. Unpleasantly warm flesh. Straying elbows that carelessly jabbed into her ribs. She froze as a new sensation invaded the normal crush. The back of her skull prickled at the gentle scrape of fingernails. The doors opened just as she tried to turn. Cool night air chilled her skin as the flow of the crowd pushed her forward. With renewed determination to avoid whoever was on the train, she gathered her hair over one shoulder and ignored the retreating touch.

Moving swiftly to avoid being consumed by the flowing crowd, she passed alongside the train, heading towards the exit stairs. The lights of the train and overhead fluorescents beat back the night as best they could. Still, dark shadows were splayed across the ground and walls. Each one weaker than the figure she had spotted before but enough to make her flinch. She kept her gaze locked straight ahead. It didn't stop her attention being captured by the figure again. It flicked across the corner of her eyes, gone almost as quickly as she spotted it. But the sensation of being watched lingered. It played across her skin like a wave of needles. Gathering her coat tightly around herself, she rushed up the stairs.

Reaching the bridge that arched over the rails didn't extinguish the sensation, only lessened it. Keeping a brisk pace, she adjusted her purse strap and took a sobering breath of the night air. Still, a cold lump formed in the pit of her stomach, making it a struggle to keep her head high. A part of her wanted to look back. But humoring the sensation would only give it meaning. So she focused instead on getting away from the station and clearing her mind. Each step brought a dull throb of pain as her work shoes rubbed against her heels. It made her wince as she took the flight of stairs down to get back onto street level.

Soon.

She whipped around as the single whispered word hit her ears. One hand had shot out to grip the railing. A chill lingered to the metal and worked its way into her palm as she searched the faces of the people shuffling to get around her. None of them acknowledged her beyond a slight glance of annoyance. A gentle breeze blew again, and she convinced herself that was all it was. A strange phenomenon caused by fraying nerves.

Nothing more.

Swallowing thickly, she turned back around and continued on her way.

This side of the station was almost as populated as the train itself. Traffic was a steady strum through the streets while both sides were filled with restaurants and bars. As her fellow travelers dispersed around her, they were near instantly replaced with people searching for their friends or food. Different scents filled the air, reminding her of how hungry she was. Weaving through the crowd, she twisted to avoid a couple that had suddenly stopped short. That's when she noticed the figure from the train. It remained still as the world seemed to swirl around it. She only had a split second to recognize that it was there before the crowd swallowed it back up and she lost sight of it again.

People bumped into her, shoving her back and forth, snapping her out of her shocked stupor. Clutching her bag to her side, she rushed forward with renewed determination. Her skin crawled over her bones. Her heart beat wildly around her chest even as she struggled to dismiss the figure as merely a trick of the light.

For two streets, moving through the crowd was like pushing against a tide. The relatively short distance took far too long. She just wanted to be home. Finally, making it to the corner where the stoplight made it possible to cross the road, she joined the crowd already massing. Once more, people pushed in around her. But without the confines of a train, they were able to keep a little more distance between each other. She knew this logically. That didn't stop her from feeling like they were only a breath away from her back. She could almost feel the heat of someone's hand hovering between her shoulder blades. Twitching as if she could physically dislodge the sensation, she pushed her hair over her shoulder. Just the barest of a turn and it was there again. Lurking in the corner of her eyes.

Her spine straightened. The figure was closer than it had been before, but still had no real detail. No hair or arms or face. It was nothing more than an ebony smear in the edges of her peripheral vision. As subtly as she could, she shifted, fussing with her purse strap for an excuse to look back. A spike of fear lodged in her lungs as the thought bubbled into her mind that her pursuer would be encouraged by any form of acknowledgment.

Keeping to her ruse, she fiddled with her shirt as she turned a little more. But as she tried to inch the figure out of the corner of her eyes, it drifted. Explanations and excuses flooded her mind as to why the figure would do this but none of them were comforting. She struggled to keep her breathing even as the point of darkness seeped behind her, only to reemerge and settle once more on the very edge of her blind spot.

Soon.

The word froze her blood as the walk light flicked on. The raspy voice echoed with a chilling certainty in her ears, making sure that she had heard it. She raced forward, pushing her way past a few people in front of her. Angry grunts followed her. A few muttered words. She didn't pay attention to either. Her nerve endings felt like live wires, each one screaming at her to get some distance from her pursuer. But there was a price to pay. As she neared her home, the stores grew scarce, the streetlights more scattered, and the crowds thinned. Without the competing noise, she could hear how labored her breathing was. The hitch and strain. It created a self-fulfilling loop, the sound feeding her fear and making her breath harder.

Her shoes clicked against the sidewalk. A quick, repetitive rhythm that bounced off of the surrounding buildings. Gradually, the beat changed. Doubled. Signaling that someone else was on the street behind her. It started as a scraping shuffle. Barely distinguishable under her own rapid pace. Soon it was louder, closer. Not daring to look behind, she walked faster. The shuffle matched her pace. Every heartbeat hurt, pounding like a drum, urging her to run. Her skin tightened over her bones and her muscles twitched but she kept her pace, her eyes locked on the approaching street corner.

As calmly as she could, she turned the corner. The instant the brick edge worked to hide her from her follower's sight, she broke into a sprint.

Her lungs burned within moments. The pain swept into her legs soon after. But she kept pushing forward, clutching her bag to her chest to keep it from battering against her side or being used as a handle to drag her back. The shuffle became a lumbering scrape. For all that it sounded like the figure was hobbling, it was fast. No matter how hard she pushed herself, it was a losing battle to keep her lead. The scrape drew nearer, grew louder, the sound driving her into a blinding panic.

Racing around another corner, she spotted her apartment building in the distance. Lights shone in the windows like beacons, promising safety, sanctuary. She shoved her hand into her purse and scrambled for her keys. Clutched the slips of metal until they dug into her palm. It occurred to her between heartbeats that she was leading the figure right to her home, but fear kept her barreling towards the building.

The shuffling, scraping, lurching footsteps grew closer. Closer. Haggard breathing that wasn't her own filled her ears. Hot breath pushed against the back of her neck. With a shattered cry, she whipped around and slashed her hand out, using the keys as knife. They met no resistance. Her hand was left to fall uselessly to her side as she stared down the dark, deserted street. Noises drifted to her from the restaurants. The general buzz of surrounding life hovered around her. But the street itself was empty.

Shaken, she rushed up the staircase and pushed her way through the security door. As it clicked shut behind her, the little whirl of machinery telling her that the lock had fastened, she let out a sigh of relief. The small, annoying rub of her shoes had turned into a painful fire after the run. So she slipped her shoes off before climbing the long, narrow stretch of stairs. It was a hard slog to make it up the flight. Her legs were heavy and her lungs burned. Reaching the landing, she turned to go down the hall. That's when she saw it. A patch of black standing at the base of the stairs.

Pain forgotten, she raced down the hallway, fingers fumbling with her apartment keys. The slow, steady shuffle of feet climbed the stairs behind her. At her door, her hands shaking, unable to fit the key into the lock, she glanced back. The hallway was empty. The shuffling continued. She looked back at the door, desperate to fit the key. It was there. In the corner of her eyes. The edge of her vision. She snapped her head up, a scream lingering on the tip of her tongue but failing to come.

The hallway was empty. Silent but for the scratches of her key searching for the lock. The abrupt jerk of it slipping it into place lurched her forward, her shoulder smacking against the door.

Now.

Her gaze shot towards the noise. It was there, standing beside her, filling her peripheral vision with an inky black. She tried to jerk away but found herself frozen in place. Her mind screamed to move, to run, but her muscles wouldn't listen. Each one locked into place as the dark mass spread out within the edges of her vision. It surrounded her. Engulfed her. Hot breath washed over her trembling skin as her field of vision narrowed. Breaking through her shock, she opened her mouth to scream. The darkness rushed forward, latching onto her like thousands of hands that would not let go. She felt herself sucked into it, and she kicked and struggled against the pull. The darkness enveloped her, crawled into her open mouth and stung her eyes as the invisible hands pulled her in and dragged her down into the bottomless abyss.

Her scream died as swiftly as it began, leaving only the rattle of her keys swinging in the lock to break the silence of the now empty hallway. The overhead lights burned brightly, chasing away the calm night, ensuring that the shadows could exist only within the corners.

* * *

The Sins We Hide
By A. I. Nasser

The night I found Ashley Cooper, I almost killed her.

She was standing in the middle of the road, arms hanging by her side, hair falling down to her shoulders and damp, as if she had just stepped out of the shower and had thought it a good idea to take a midnight stroll down Helmen Drive. As if she had somehow lost her way and had reverted to extreme measures just to get someone's attention.

As if she hadn't been missing for four years.

Four years.

People say nothing ever happens in Loster, Connecticut, and I used to believe that. A long time ago. When being the Sheriff of this small town involved nothing more than handling disputes between neighbors and the occasional drunk driver—usually Jim Haze, and always on Sunday night when he'd lose at a game of cards.

Not that I was complaining. I loved small town law. Two deputies, Martha on the phone, and I was usually back home a bit after sunset with a six-pack and a few hours in front of the TV to look forward to. Every now and then I'd get called back in; never anything serious, but enough of a ruckus to warrant a visit by yours truly. I can remember every time that had happened, mainly because I could count them on the fingers of one hand.

It was routine, really. Wake up, drive the narrow road into town, pick up a bagel and coffee, and end up behind my desk with time to kill. Paperwork was probably the only thing that kept any of us awake, and the routes of course. Four of them, every three hours, letting the little over two thousand law-abiding citizens of Loster know that we were still there, keeping them safe.

Not that they needed it. The people of Loster were a God-fearing bunch, and every Sunday morning I'd get a call from Pastor Charles Gate, asking if I'd be joining the congregation that week. That my presence would really be missed, and it would be nice to see the familiar face of the law sitting between everyone else in the pews. I'd always thank him, tell him I would try to make it. I never did, though. I had given up on religion the day my daughter died. I wasn't interested in finding God. I had a beef with Him, and I had a feeling we weren't going to really hit it off if I ever set foot in Loster's First.

What I usually ended up doing on Sunday was spend the evening and the better part of the night at Joe's, talking about the Red Sox and trying my best not to call my ex-wife. Never drinking, though. The ride home was long, and Helmen Drive was known for a few twists and turns that always took you by surprise. Not to mention the occasional deer, or if you're really lucky, a parked car with two teenagers inside who had somehow decided that making out in the middle of nowhere was a smart idea.

I liked my routine. It gave me structure, and after Holly's death, I needed a lot more of that than usual. It was hard coming to terms with cancer, and even harder to think that a six-year-old should suffer and die the way she had. Structure was good. Routine was important. Without it, I'd have put a gun to my head a long time ago and pulled the trigger.

The night I almost ran over Ashley Cooper, standing in the middle of Helmen Drive where no person in their right mind should be standing, that structure was shattered. Along with my windshield and the front half of my truck after I had hit the tree, swerving to avoid her.

Four years.

It had been one of the rare occasions I had been called back into the station. The Coopers had reported their six-year-old missing, again, and knowing little Ashley, we hadn't been too worried. Everyone knew how adventurous she was, a mini thrill-seeker with an affinity for the woods behind town. The last time she had gone missing, we had found her by the lake at the edge of the woods, skipping rocks and smiling at the ripples they made. I had made that my first stop, and when I didn't find her, had taken to the woods with the others.

By day two, we had called in reinforcements. Divers in the lake, dogs after her scent, and her picture faxed to every station in the neighboring towns.

By week two, everyone across the nation knew Ashley Cooper's name and face, and I had even come across websites created for what had become the 'Search for Loster's Lost Child'.

We held a funeral for her after three months, when the Coopers had given up completely and winter had come rolling in. I had attended the funeral, had watched Susan Cooper cry a river, holding her husband's arm as he stared off into space as if he were somewhere else. The only one who had really been *there*, was Nancy. The older sister. The high school valedictorian who had been just a few months away from a future at Harvard.

Loster had given up on Ashley, but I hadn't. I had spent the rest of the year looking, following any leads, asking around and using all the favors I had with anyone who could point me in the right direction. And still nothing. On the anniversary of her disappearance, I had finally joined the fold, and for the first time since the funeral, visited her grave and apologized.

Four years.

She came back after four years, and I almost killed her.

***

"Cuts and bruises, Sheriff Barker."

Doctor Emily Lewis looked up from the chart in her hands, gave me a quick smile, then went back to jotting things down.

She'd been responsible for the Loster Medical Center for over a decade now, and she ran it the way she would a fully functioning hospital. So well, in fact, that most of the neighboring towns poured into Loster first, taking her and her staff's recommendations before being transferred somewhere else if needed. She made my job easier, and over the years, we had built a sort of repertoire that had quickly turned into a strong friendship. Her support during Holly's sickness had been one of the reasons I was still a sane man.

It didn't mean we never bumped heads. It was part of the charm, really. Like a game of chess, with each one of us trying to enforce our jurisdiction over the other.

She usually won.

"I feel like I shattered a collar bone," I said, wincing as I pulled my coat on. The Sheriff's emblem was stitched on, with a brownish shade that made its original yellow color almost obsolete. I felt it was a quaint reflection of the man wearing it.

"X-rays are clean," Emily said. "Unless you want to make the drive into Hartford and get us a CT. I don't think you need one, but hey, if you haven't had enough excitement for one night, knock yourself out."

"And the girl?" I asked. "Ashley?"

The interval between climbing out of my truck and calling in back-up was a bit of a blur. All I remember was damp earth, coughing and gasping for breath, and an incredible amount of pain. And Ashley, of course. Standing next to me when I finally looked up, scaring the hell out of me with that stare of hers and the hair that stuck to her face and neck like a second layer of skin. I remember whispering her name, coaxing her into saying anything at all, but all I got was the stare. Eyes following me as I moved, always only a few feet away from me while we waited for the ambulance to pick us up.

"You need to stop calling her that," Emily said. "You already got the paramedics spooked."

"Come on, doc, that's Ashley Cooper," I said. "You know that better than I do."

"Hell of a resemblance, sure," Emily nodded. "But we're running DNA tests, and we'll see what comes back. How long has it been?"

Four years.

"Too long," I said. "I need to call her parents."

"You definitely do not," Emily said, dropping the chart on my bed and giving me a cold glare that usually preluded an argument. "Dennis Barker you will not give these people false hope."

"That's Ashley Cooper!" I almost yelled.

Emily looked around her before pulling the curtains closed around us. "Dennis, that is a little *girl*. A very frightened, admittedly creepy, little girl who is in severe shock. She hasn't said a word since she's come in, and all I could tell by going over the scratches and bruises on her body was that she must have been in those damn woods for a very long time."

"Exactly," I said. "Whoever took her, she must have gotten away. Tried to find her way home. Came to the only place she knew."

"That's just one theory," Emily argued. "Another is that this is a girl who looks a lot like little Ashley, or at least what she would have looked like if we had watched her grow up, and has been lost in those woods for days. Maybe her parents are looking for her? Don't you think that's a possibility?"

"Doc, you can't be serious."

"Listen, all I'm asking is for you to wait for the DNA tests," Emily said. "Two days, tops. We'll keep a lid on things until then. For now she's just Jane Doe."

I had half a mind to pull my jurisdiction card, but decided that this was probably for the best. Emily was right; the girl was definitely in shock. Telling her parents would only result in a bombardment of emotions she might not be able to handle right now. Not to mention, everyone else in town would want to come see her, and the news vans would follow.

I sighed. "Fine, we'll do it your way," I gave in. "But the minute those tests come back, I'm the first one you call."

"Of course," Emily smiled.

I stood up, winced again at the pain radiating from my shoulder down my arm, and grabbed my hat. "Always good seeing you, doc."

"Don't be a stranger," Emily said as I walked past her.

I signed my release forms and left.

***

"So, was it a deer?"

I looked up from behind my desk, the reports from the other day scattered in front of me, my mind foggy. I had slept very little, constantly dreaming of little Ashley standing in the middle of Helmen Drive bathed in my truck's headlights, staring me down. Her eyes were a strange dark obsidian, and her hair seemed to crawl across her skin, as if alive. I'd swerve, crash and then wake up with a start. Sweating. Gasping for breath. My shoulder screaming.

When I'd finally fall asleep again, I'd just get a repeat of the same thing. Over and over, like a film stuck on replay. It kept me up all night.

"Hmm?"

"A deer," Dan Wilkins said, smiling. "Bastards have a death wish, then. Always prancing about as if they own the damn place."

I sighed, pinched the bridge of my nose, and shook my head at my deputy. "No, wasn't a deer."

"Fox, then?"

"Not a fox," I replied. "I think I just slept at the wheel."

"Gotta be careful 'bout that, Sheriff," Dan said, shaking his head and clicking his tongue. "Had a cousin who fell asleep at the wheel, God bless his soul."

"Thanks, Dan," I said with a weak smile. "I'll keep that in mind."

Dan gave me a thumbs-up and made to leave, when he remembered something and turned back. "By the way, Doc Emily called in a few minutes ago. Said it was important."

I was instantly alert. Didn't she say it would be two days?

"Message for me?"

"Nope," Dan shook his head. "Said she needed to see you urgently down at the clinic."

I stood up, grabbed my hat, and raced out the door.

***

One of the things about Loster I loved the most was how small the town was. The houses were scattered in small clusters around a town center that consisted of only three streets with everything crowded next to each other. It brought the community together, I felt, and gave it a kind of charm I had never felt anywhere else.

Garvey Road lead out of the town center for a few miles north, all the way to an old research facility that had once belonged to the military but had been shut down for years now. There had been talk about turning it into a college, but I doubted that would happen. Besides, a college meant more work for me, and I was quite happy with my current workload.

For a long time, Garvey Road had been closed off to stop kids from riding their bikes to the facility, daring each other to explore the place's labyrinth halls and underground labs. Too many accidents had taught us that what was abandoned should be left abandoned. The barricades were removed when old man Chester donated a piece of arid farmland to the town to build Loster Medical, but it didn't change the fact that the road remained relatively empty.

Not this morning, though.

It wasn't even noon yet, and for the entire mile's stretch it took me to reach the Medical Center, the road was packed with news vans parked one after the other. Several reporters were standing in front of cameras, microphones in their hands and fake smiles plastered across their faces. Others had made their way to the medical center itself, and were being held back by a few of the nurses and security guards.

"Shit!" I cursed under my breath as I pulled up in front of the center and turned off the engine.

A few reporters had spotted me, and through a volley of shouts and waves, the horde made its way towards me. I stepped out, cursing again, and began to force my way towards the doors.

"Sheriff, is it true that Ashley Cooper has been found?"

"Who found her?"

"Is she hurt? Do you know who took her?"

"Why won't they let us into the hospital, Sheriff? We have a right to—"

I pushed my way through the sliding glass doors and immediately called in for backup. The nurses weren't going to be able to hold them off for long, and we were going to need all the help we could get. Emily appeared before I could even make my way to the front desk.

"What did we agree to?" she snapped.

"Hey, this wasn't me," I said. "I kept my mouth shut. You should ask your staff."

"Great, Barker," Emily threw her hands up in frustration. "This is exactly what I wanted to avoid."

"Dan and Steven will be here in a bit," I tried to assure her. "We'll make sure they stay outside."

"That's not why I called," Emily said, grabbing me by the arm and pulling me along with her.

"What is it?"

"The girl," Emily said. "She's talking."

***

There was no doubt in my mind that she was Ashley Cooper.

She sat in the hospital bed, clad in a gown that made her look like she was six again. Her dark brown hair looked a lot less creepy now that it had been combed and pulled back in a loose ponytail, and her eyes had lost that forlorn look she had when I had first brought her in. I smiled at her through the window as I walked past her room, and she smiled back and waved.

"She seems good," I said.

Emily stopped me before we went in, and her voice dropped to a whisper. "First of all, the DNA tests are not back yet, but from our brief conversation, she says her name is Ashley. She's been asking for Susan and Nick incessantly, but I haven't called them."

"Still not one hundred percent sure, huh?" I asked, looking through the window and keeping my smile in place.

"I've heard of these things before," Emily said. "Family loses a child, an imposter shows up years later."

"Yeah, but they're usually a lot older when they do," I replied. "And usually it's about the money. Even if that's not Ashley, what's she going to do? Rob them while they sleep?"

"Just be careful, okay," Emily said. "Besides, she's been acting weird, too. Wants the blinds drawn all the time, no lights. She turns on the water in the bathroom and leaves it running, says it calms her or something."

I looked back at Ashley, and her smile had disappeared. She was watching us intently, as if she could somehow read our lips and know what we were saying. Her eyes bore into mine, and for a split second, I felt my skin crawl. It was funny how my feelings towards her could change in the span of a minute.

I turned my back to the window.

"It could just be PTSD," Emily was saying. "But it's just odd. I don't like it."

"The important thing is she's talking," I said. "We'll figure this all out."

"Are we bringing in the parents?"

"I'll have to if she wants to see them." I replied. "That's if those vultures outside haven't already spread the news."

As if on cue, we heard shouting from the lobby. Someone was yelling at one of the nurses to let her through. Nancy Cooper made her way around the corner, fighting her way out of the nurse's grip, and ran down the hall. I stood in her way, trying to stop her, but she was already past me and looking through the window at her sister.

"Oh my God!" she whispered. Her knees buckled, and I quickly wrapped an arm around her waist, holding her up. "Oh my God, it's true!"

Nancy pushed out of my grip and made for the door.

"Nancy—" Emily tried to stop her, but it was already too late.

Nancy Cooper already had her sister in her arms.

"I guess you don't need to call them after all," Emily whispered.

I nodded, but couldn't tear my eyes away from Ashley as she returned her sister's hug while staring directly at me.

***

"That is not my daughter!" Susan screamed.

We sat in a small waiting room on the second floor of the medical center. Nick was staring out the window, that same look on his face that he had had the day of the funeral. His lips moved. He wasn't saying anything out loud, but it definitely looked like he was having a heated argument with some other voice in his head.

Susan paced back and forth, hair disheveled, a look of shock and worry all over her face. They had arrived a few minutes after Nancy, and the first thing Susan Cooper had done was slap me. Hard. Then she started bombarding me with accusations. That I was a terrible man to give them hope like that. That I had no right to play with people's emotions in that way. It was only after we had calmed her down that she had gone on a rampage about how the girl in that room was not her daughter.

"Susan, please—"

"Shut up, Barker!" the woman screamed, pointing an angry finger at me. "You... you... I could kill you!"

"Mrs. Cooper," Emily began. "If you'd hear us out."

"Why the hell did you even tell anyone who she was?" Susan asked, her voice shrill in the small room. "If you were so sure that she was Ashley, why didn't you call us first?"

"I wanted to," I said, shooting Emily a look. "We wanted to be sure, first. Dr. Lewis was running some DNA tests. I was waiting for the results."

"That's not what those ... those ... those *monsters* outside were raving about!" Susan's eyes were full of rage, and she looked at me the way a feral animal would its prey. If given a chance, she would have ripped my heart out with her bare hands.

"Susan, you need to calm down," I said.

"Calm down? Really, Barker?" Susan hissed. "We hear that our daughter is back, we drive like maniacs all the way over here, and in the end, that *person* is sitting in a hospital bed, claiming to be my Ashley?"

"She can claim whatever she wants to claim," I said, my own voice rising, deciding enough was enough. "I already told you that we're doing the tests, and we'll find out soon enough who she really is. She had me fooled, and she's definitely got Nancy fooled."

"She's not fooling me!" Susan snapped.

"Fine," I shot back. "Then go home, and wait for my call."

Susan looked like she was about to say something snappy back, but thought better of it and slumped down in a chair. She looked at her husband, realized he wasn't going to take her side, or anyone else's for that matter, and dropped her head.

"How long?"

We all turned to Nick who had finally decided to join the party.

"Excuse me?" Emily asked.

"How long before the tests come back?"

She looked at her watch and shrugged. "I asked them to hurry it up for me," she said. "The soonest they'll be able to get back to me is in an hour."

Nick nodded, not turning around, standing in that same stoic pose as he stared out the window. "Fine," he said. "We'll wait."

I caught Susan look at him, then turn away again. The frown on her face was a clear indication as to how she felt about that.

"Could you do me a favor, Sheriff?"

"Sure, Nick, whatever you need." I kept my eyes on Susan, though. Her erratic behavior had me on edge, and I didn't need the extra strain on my nerves.

"Make sure the reporters don't get in," Nick said. "And keep an eye on Nancy for us?"

I turned to Emily and raised an eyebrow. When she nodded that she'd be okay alone with the two of them, I turned and left the room.

The walk back took forever. Suddenly, my feet felt like lead, slowing me down and making every step feel like a strained effort. Thoughts circled through my head, an inexplicable dread I couldn't place. I had been so sure. How could I have been wrong?

A part of me tried to concentrate on the fact that even Nancy was convinced the girl was her sister. But it was Susan's reaction that worried me. A mother would know her daughter; I was convinced of that. If Susan said the girl wasn't Ashley, then she probably wasn't.

So who the hell was she?

I knocked before finally pushing into the hospital room. Nancy was lying on the bed next to our Jane Doe, holding her in her arms. The girl was asleep, and Nancy quickly put a finger to her lips when I came in. I lifted both hands up and started to retreat when my foot kicked the table.

Ashley's eyes flew open immediately, and she quickly sat up, her gaze freezing me in place.

"Sorry," I grimaced. "Didn't mean to wake you up."

"That's okay," Nancy said when Ashley didn't reply right away. "She's been asleep for a while anyway."

"How are you, sweetheart?" I asked, pulling up a chair next to the bed, but still keeping a safe enough distance away. *She's just a girl. What the hell are you afraid of?*

The eyes. Those twin blues that stared at me as if stripping me of my skin and peeking into the depths of my soul.

Nancy patted the girl on the head and gave her a quick squeeze. "It's okay, Ashley," she said. "You remember Sheriff Barker, right?"

Ashley nodded but didn't say anything. She looked at her sister, then back at me.

"I heard you've started talking," I nudged. "That's great. Real great. I bet you've got a lot of stories to tell."

Ashley cocked her head to one side, and for a second I could have sworn those blues had turned a darker shade. "I want mommy," she finally said.

Her voice was a little hoarse, barely a whisper, but cut through me like a thousand little knives. Almost like nails scratching across a chalkboard. I winced, quickly tried to hide it, but could see she had noticed.

"I want mommy," she repeated.

"Sure, sweetie," I replied, forcing a smile. "She's actually here. We just need her to fill out a bunch of paperwork before she can come and see you. Get that stuff out of the way so you could have her all to yourself."

Ashley returned my smile, and I felt my mind scream. It wasn't the sweet smile of a ten-year-old. There was something there. Something very, very wrong.

"All to myself," Ashley said. "I'd like that."

***

Emily saved me after about twenty minutes of awkward chitchat and me pretending that everything was fine with the world.

She came into the room, claimed that the deputies were asking for me, and gave the sisters one of those smiles doctors saved for patients when they didn't want them to know that something was wrong. She couldn't have picked a better time. I had already started to feel incredibly uncomfortable, and had no idea what excuse I could use to leave. Ashley had spent the entire time staring at me, saying very little, and asking for her mother. I was a few seconds away from screaming at her to just shut up and stop looking at me like that. It made my skin crawl.

I started making my way to the front lobby, but Emily grabbed my arm and pulled me in the opposite direction. I followed her silently, a little confused, but mostly worried. She looked pale, and she kept looking over her shoulder as if expecting someone to be following us. She led me to the lab, ushered me inside and closed the door behind us.

"She's definitely Ashley Cooper," she said after making sure the door was locked.

"What?" The news hit me like a wrecking ball. I had been ready to believe I was wrong, especially after the way Susan had reacted.

"The lab in Hartford called me," Emily said. "They're still writing the report and will email it to me in a bit, but they knew I was in a hurry. She's an exact match, Barker. She's Ashley."

"Then what the hell was Susan's reaction all about?" I asked.

Emily shrugged and shook her head. "I have no idea," she said. "Denial maybe? She's spent the past four years thinking her daughter was dead, and then last night she just suddenly appears out of nowhere. That's definitely got to be hard for her."

"That makes no sense," I said. "She'd know her own goddamn daughter."

"What are you so worked up about?" Emily frowned. "You're the one who was so sure it was Ashley. I would've expected you to be a little happier."

"Same back at ya," I said.

"I am happy," Emily shot, but her eyes said different.

"Then why bring me here?" I asked. "Locked door, empty lab?"

Emily opened her mouth to reply, then closed it.

"You feel it, too, don't you?" I said.

"Something's just not right with that girl, Barker," she said. "Even if she is Ashley."

I sighed. I felt it, too, but just couldn't place it.

"What do we do?" Emily asked.

"Nothing," I said. "We need to tell Nick and Susan that their daughter's come home."

"I don't want to be in the room when we tell Susan."

"Yeah. Me neither."

***

Susan went ballistic.

To say she wasn't happy about what we had to tell her was an understatement. Emily had taken it upon herself to be the bearer of the news, and Susan had reacted with a flurry of insults and accusations that would have made a sailor blush. That was closely followed by screaming fits that could have shattered glass, and no matter what I tried to say to calm her down, it only made her angrier.

Nick had come out of his stupor long enough to make us repeat the fact that Ashley really was in a hospital bed downstairs over a dozen times. In the midst of his wife's screaming and shouting, he had made his way to a corner and had sat down heavily on the floor, his hands covering his face as he rocked back and forth.

It was the strangest thing I had ever experienced, and that was even after my short conversation with Ashley that had given me the jitters. A part of me wanted to grab each one in turn and shake some sense into them. To tell them that this was a good thing; that their daughter who everyone had assumed was dead, was back. They had a second chance. Something that not everyone got. Something I personally would have killed for.

But I didn't do that. I couldn't. Just watching them react to the news had frozen me in place, and it took a few minutes before I realized that my hand had subconsciously dropped to my revolver. Emily looked ashen, but stood her ground. Her lips were pressed into a very thin line, and she held her head high, ready for anything the Coopers had to throw at her. It took guts and a hell of a lot of confidence to pull that off, and I felt a tinge of pride as I looked at her from the corner of my eye.

Susan eventually calmed down, slumped in her chair, exhausted, crying openly. She looked like a defeated woman, and a part of me wanted to take the seat beside her, wrap an arm around her shoulder and tell her that everything would be alright. But the other part of me, the one angry at their blatant ungratefulness, kept me rooted in place. For a second, even the thought of how much they didn't deserve this second chance at a life with their daughter crossed my mind. I quickly pushed that away.

We spent another hour with them in the waiting room, saying nothing, patiently letting the news sink in. When Nick finally got up, he made his way out of the waiting room and disappeared down the hall. Emily gave me a concerned look, and I nodded to her to follow him.

"You don't have to stay with me, Sheriff," Susan said after a few more minutes of silence.

I shrugged. "You look like you need the company."

She scoffed. "You probably think I'm a terrible mother."

"I won't lie to you, the thought's crossed my mind," I said.

She looked at me, but I didn't meet her gaze, keeping my eyes focused on the door and the empty hall beyond.

"I don't care what the tests say, Barker," she said. "That's not Ashley. That's not my daughter."

I turned to her then, barely controlling my anger, and took one of her hands in mine. "I'm not going to pretend that I know what you're going through right now," I said. "But believe me when I tell you I know what you went through four years ago. I know the pain of losing a child, what that does to you. How it tears a family apart from the inside out. I lost everything when Holly died, Susan. Everything. I fell into this hole, this dark, abyss of a hole that I couldn't climb out of. It destroyed my marriage, and pretty much everything else." I squeezed her hand hard. "You just got your little girl back. Think about that for a second before you say something stupid like that again."

She looked at me, tears rolling down her cheeks, lips quivering. "You don't understand."

"Do you?" I asked. "That girl downstairs, she misses her mother. She's been asking about you ever since she started talking. You need to see her, Susan."

She shook her head frantically, pulled her hand out from between mine, and quickly stood up. "No," she said. "No, I can't. I can't."

She repeated it like a mantra, walking to a corner where she wrapped her arms around her body and began to cry again. I sighed, stood up and was about to go to her when Nancy came in.

"Mom?"

Susan turned, and with tears, rushed up to her daughter and hugged her. Nancy's eyes grew wide in surprise, and she looked at me for an explanation.

"She's a little emotional," I played it down.

Nancy's frown deepened, and she hugged her mother back. "Mom, what's wrong?"

"Who's with Ashley?" I asked.

"No one," Nancy replied. "She fell asleep, so I came up here to see what was going on."

"I'll keep an eye on her," I sighed. "You take care of your mother. Talk some sense into her."

I left the waiting room and leaned against the corridor wall. Feeling a little defeated, I took off my hat and ran a hand through my hair.

Then the lights went out.

***

"What's going on?"

Nancy came running out of the waiting room just as the emergency lights came on, dousing the corridor in a sickening red light.

"Not sure," I said, waiting for my eyes to adjust. "Power outage, probably. The generators should kick in any second now."

"Okay," she said, looking a little perplexed by this. "I can't remember the last time we had a power outage in Loster."

Neither could I, and the fact that the generators hadn't started running yet confused me even more. "I'll go check on Ashley," I said.

"I'm coming with you."

"No, you stay with your mother," I said, already making my way towards the stairs at the end of the corridor.

"She's a big girl, Sheriff," Nancy said, catching up to me as we descended to the first floor.

We ran into Emily and Nick just as we rounded a corner, apparently on their way to us.

"Why aren't the generators working?" I asked.

"No idea," Emily said. "We were supposed to have them replaced months ago, but you know Jim. Takes forever to get anything done."

I clicked my tongue and pushed past them towards Ashley's room. "You should check on the other patients," I said.

"What do you think this is, Hartford?" Emily asked. "The center's empty except for Ashley."

"I think I should be grateful about that."

"Where's Susan?" Nick asked.

"Upstairs," I replied. "Do me a favor, take Nancy and go stay with her. I'll be up in a few." Nancy was about to protest, but I wasn't having it. "Go, already!"

I waited until they disappeared around a corner, then turned to Emily. "Find Jim and get this place running again," I said. "These red lights are creeping the hell out of me."

Emily nodded and rushed towards the main lobby.

I walked in the opposite direction, making my way to Ashley's room, hoping she hadn't been scared senseless by the blackout. Creepy or not, she was still just a little girl, and if her mother didn't want to be with her, I was definitely not going to leave her alone.

Thinking about what I would say to keep the girl calm and preoccupied, I rounded a corner and came to a sudden stop.

Ashley Cooper was standing in the middle of the corridor, just outside her room, looking very much the same way she had when I had first found her. Her hair was matted against her scalp, the dampness darkening the top of her hospital gown, and her eyes glistened in the red light. She looked like she was lost, her head turning in circles, as if she were trying to figure out where she was.

"Ashley?" I called out.

She turned to me, and I felt my heart skip a beat. Her eyes had lost all their color, a complete black that made me feel like I was looking into a pair of bottomless pits. Her hands twitched and she cocked her head to a side, the same way she had before. Only this time, it seemed like it was an involuntary reaction, as if her head were too heavy for her neck to carry.

But what really made my blood freeze and my entire body go cold was her smile. That sickening, dark smile.

"All to myself," she said in a voice so deep, it didn't feel like it was hers.

The emergency lights went out and I couldn't see a damn thing.

I quickly reached for my flashlight and brought it up, aiming the beam at where I had last seen Ashley. But she was gone.

That's when the screaming began.

***

I almost ran into Emily at the base of the staircase, the emergency lights going out everywhere, one by one. I could barely see her, but her face reflected everything I was thinking. The screaming was coming from upstairs, from the waiting room.

I took the stairs by two, not caring if Emily was close behind or not. My revolver was out, held tight in both hands as I raced down the second floor corridor. I almost shot Nancy when she ran around the corner and practically threw herself into my arms.

"Mom!" she was screaming. "Mom!"

I made sure Emily had caught up before I left Nancy with her and ran towards the waiting room. Nick was waiting outside, staring into the room with wide eyes and his mouth hanging open. I pushed past him, storming into the room just as the power came back on and the lights flickered back to life.

I would have lost my mind if it hadn't been for Emily rushing to my side and letting out a small shriek of her own. One she quickly stifled as we both tried to make sense of what we were looking at.

Susan Cooper sat in a chair staring back at us with lifeless eyes. Her mouth hung open and to one side, as if it had somehow lost touch with which way was down and had decided to try a different route. Her fingers had dug into the armrests so hard that several nails had broken and blood was oozing down the side of the chair.

What made the whole thing worse was that she wasn't alone. Standing by her side, head hanging low and shoulders moving up and down as she sobbed, was Ashley.

She looked up at us, and for a second, I saw the same black orbs that had gazed at me just seconds ago. They quickly transformed into her baby blues, and the tears streaming down her face could have been heart wrenching if I didn't feel like a cold hand had found its way to my spine and was twisting hard.

"I wanted to see my mama," Ashley was saying.

"Oh God, Barker, get her out," Emily gasped, pushing past me and quickly wrapping the little girl in her arms. She twisted her away from the scene of her dead mother and quickly began soothing her.

You haven't seen her, Emily. You don't know what you're holding. That really isn't Ashley Cooper. Susan was right, Emily. We were wrong, and she was right!

I snapped out of my daze, slipped the revolver into its holster, and took a few steps towards Susan's lifeless body. I put a hand to her neck, confirming what I already knew.

"Doc," I whispered. "I think this is your territory."

When Emily didn't reply, I looked at her. She was staring at Susan with a mix of horror and confusion, as if trying to make sense of what had happened.

"Doc!"

Emily blinked twice and shook her head. "Take Ashley," she said.

I took a tentative step back, and was rewarded with a frown from Emily. "Nancy?" I called out. "Nancy, come take your sister. She shouldn't be in here."

Emily didn't wait for the older girl to come in, and she led Ashley out, leaving me alone with Susan. I leaned forward, slowly closing her eyes, worried that she might just decide to come back and bite my hand off. I could almost see it happening, and why the hell not? I was seeing a hell of a lot of strange things lately.

I turned to Nick who was still standing at the door. "Jesus Christ, what just happened?"

Nick didn't reply. Emily came back in with her stethoscope and bent over Susan, trying to hear for even the faintest sign of a pulse. I could see her squinting, concentrating, the doctor in her hoping that she could still save the woman. After a few seconds, she stood back up and shook her head.

"Someone tell me something," I demanded. "She was perfectly fine when I left her."

"I don't know, Barker," Emily said. "What I want to know is how Ashley got up here."

"What do you mean?"

"There's only one way up, and one corridor from her room to here. How did you not see her?"

"The lights went out," I said. "Really? That's what's bothering you?"

"The girl's been through enough shock, and now her mother's dead," Emily shouted. "Yes, Sheriff, that's what's bothering me."

"Then why don't you ask her?" I yelled back. "Christ, Emily, I have no idea."

"I do," Nick said, and we both turned to look at him.

"What?"

"I know how Ashley got here," Nick said, his eyes slowly turning so that he was looking straight at me. "Sheriff, we need to talk."

***

We set up in Emily's office. I had instructed Dan and Steve to keep their eyes on Nancy and the girl who, I was now very much convinced, was *not* Ashley Cooper. She wasn't even your run of the mill imposter if I had any say in it. She was something else entirely, and that something scared me.

"All ears," I said, pulling up a chair for Emily to sit in while I leaned against the office door.

Nick sat on the couch with his hands curled up in his lap, his eyes staring down at the floor. He wet his lips, opened his mouth to talk, and then closed it again. I had a feeling we were going to lose him, and snapped my fingers to get his attention.

"Now, Nick," I said. "Come on."

Emily shot me an angry glare, and I ignored her completely, not ready to take any more crap for the night.

"You'll excuse me if I'm a little slow," Nick said. "It's going to take me a few minutes to get my head straight."

"Of course," Emily said. "Whenever you're ready."

He's never going to be truly ready. He just lost his wife.

I pushed back the cynic inside me and decided to follow Emily's lead. If Nick had answers, I wanted to hear them, and rushing him was probably going to make him shut down again.

"A few years before Ashley went missing, things at home were not going very well," Nick began. "You both know that I work as a consultant. I travel a lot, but most of the work I do is out of my office at home. Freelance consulting. I thought it would give me more time to spend with the family, but what it really does is force me to work odd hours, every day. I am constantly on call, and family time ... let's just say that almost never happened.

"Susan didn't take to it too well. She said I was working a lot more since I took on freelancing, and she resented it. A lot. So much that she started looking for comfort in our wine collection. At first, I thought it was a good thing, something to help take the edge off, keep her off my case while I finished my work. It was slow at first, but gradually became worse. The wine bottles were replaced with even more, and soon we had a collection of brandy, scotch, whiskey; a mini-bar that would have made my old man proud.

"Of course, that never helped with the anger. Her temper became worse, and once she became a full-fledged alcoholic, that anger turned into bitterness and resentment. Towards me, the girls, everyone really. She stopped seeing her friends, quit her job. She just stayed home all day, drinking."

A tear raced down one cheek, and I waited patiently as he wiped it away and tried to collect his thoughts. A part of me wondered why I had never seen it. Loster was a small town, and news travelled fast; gossip even faster. And Martha was the gossip queen. I was surprised she had never told me anything about the Coopers in the midst of all the other crap she was constantly telling me.

"It became so bad that I had stopped trying to help her and had set up in the guest room. I tried to steer clear from her, keep my distance, and I know that only made things worse. One night while I was taking the garbage out, the bag caught in the fence and tore. Everything spilled out, and right in the middle of all our trash were pill bottles. Not prescription, I could see that immediately.

"I confronted her, and she lashed out. Apparently, she had been taking oxycodone for quite some time and I had no idea. I was furious, threatened to take the girls and leave if she didn't see a specialist immediately. She got violent, broke things, and I had to leave just so she would calm down."

Nick sniffed, ran a hand through his hair, and sat back. He was crying openly now, and the pain in his eyes made my stomach turn.

"I came home one day when I thought she would be asleep. I wanted to get some of my things, and check in on the girls. She wasn't asleep, though. I walked into the house and found her sitting in the living room with a drink in her hand. Her clothes were drenched, like she had taken a shower in them, and there was this wide smile on her face that scared me to death. When I tried talking to her, she just laughed and shook her glass at me, telling me that everything was my fault. That what happened was all my fault.

"I wasn't in a mood to argue. I just wanted to take my stuff and go, and see the girls."

Nick gasped, bent over and broke into a sobbing fit. Emily leaned over, squeezing his shoulder, whispering something incoherent to him until he slowly nodded and collected himself again.

"Susan was gone. Drunk and high and making no sense. She told me Nancy was out. Study group. When I asked about Ashley, she just laughed. She went on a rambling fit about how our little girl was an ungrateful brat who just wouldn't shut up. 'She wouldn't stop asking about you,' Susan said. 'It was just so annoying,' she said. I was afraid. I knew Susan could be violent, and I was worried she had taken out her anger on our daughter. I ran up to her room. I wasn't going to leave her with Susan another night. But she wasn't in her room."

"Was that the day she disappeared?" I asked, angry as hell that Nick hadn't told me all of this four years ago. "Did she run away?"

Nick broke into tears again, and it was all I could do not to grab him by the collar of his shirt and punch his teeth out.

"Dammit, Nick, you had us thinking she's been missing for four years!" I yelled. "No wonder she's shell shocked! Did you know where she was all this time?"

Nick nodded, and Emily had to stop me from throttling him.

"You son of a bitch!" I yelled. "I spent a whole year looking for her, you bastard! A year! Where was she? Where?"

"Barker, calm down!" Emily was shouting.

"Look at me, you son of a bitch!" My voice boomed, and Nick visibly cringed as he sobbed. "Is that why you wouldn't believe she was back? Tell me!"

"No!" Nick yelled.

"What do you mean, no?" I demanded. "Are you trying to tell me you knew she'd be back?"

"No," Nick cried. "No, no, no."

"Talk!"

"She shouldn't be back!" Nick screamed. "She never ran away! She was dead, Barker, dead! Susan had drowned her in the bathtub! She was dead when I found her!"

***

I sped down Garvey Road, past the news vans, past the reporters who had set up camp all across the farmlands on either side. I drove like a bat out of hell, tires screeching as I took turns a little too quickly, engine roaring when I pushed down on the gas until the pedal had nowhere else to go.

Dan had interrupted us just as both Emily and I had been trying to swallow what Nick had told us. The moment the words had come out of the man's mouth, images of my accident flashed before my eyes. Ashley Cooper, hair wet, dark eyes staring at me. It was impossible to believe, and my mind was screaming, telling me that none of this could possibly be true.

But for some reason, it made sense. For some strange, twisted and inexplicable reason, I believed it.

I wanted to know more, but when Dan told me Ashley was missing, I forgot all about it. We searched every inch of the medical center, but she was nowhere to be found. And with only one way out, it was highly unlikely she could have slipped past the security and nurses manning the doors.

Then again, Ashley Cooper didn't travel around like the rest of us, and I had a pretty good idea where I might find her.

The cruiser was a bitch to control, and it took me forever to race past town center and towards the Coopers' old Victorian. When I finally arrived, I jumped out, left the engine running and raced into the woods behind the house.

I cut through the foliage as if I were running a marathon, barely keeping myself from falling face first every time I tripped over a fallen branch or rock lying in the way. I could feel my legs burning from exhaustion, my body protesting against the strain it was not accustomed to. But I pushed through it all, forcing myself to run faster.

I found her exactly where I expected to, standing at the edge of the lake with her feet just barely in the water.

She wasn't skipping stones this time.

"Stop right there!" I yelled, pulling my revolver out and slowing down my pace, approaching her carefully.

She turned to me, that same blood-chilling smile on her face, those damned obsidian eyes.

"I don't know who or what you are," I said, "but you're coming with me."

Ashley laughed and looked out at the lake again. "No," she said. "No, I'm not."

"You killed Susan Cooper," I said. "I have no idea how you did it, but I intend to find out."

She looked at me again, her smile wider now and gestured with her head at the lake. "My father brought me here. In a boat. Threw me over. The lake was too big for the divers to find me, but that's okay. I could find my own way out."

"Stop talking," I said. "You're not Ashley Cooper. I don't believe that story."

I was lying through my teeth, and she could tell, because the second the words left my mouth, she was giggling.

"My father was good to me," she said, her voice deepening, a hoarseness in it that made me cringe. "I don't blame him. My mother. That was different."

I was only a few feet away, and in what little light there was, I could see her skin begin to peel off. She took a step into the lake.

"Don't," I warned.

"Goodbye, Sheriff," she said. "Take care of my sister."

She giggled again, then took a few more steps into the lake until the water had reached her thighs. I raised my gun to the skies and fired a warning shot, but it didn't faze her. She kept going.

"Don't make me do this!" I called out.

She didn't answer. The water was just over her waist now, and she showed no signs of stopping.

I threw caution to the wind and fired at her. The bullet lodged in her right shoulder, but did nothing to slow her down. I fired again, and again.

By the time I was out, her head had disappeared below the surface completely, and I was left standing alone at the edge of the lake. I dropped to my knees, my eyes scanning the expanse of the body of water in front of me, looking for any sign of her.

She was gone.

* * *

If you enjoyed the book, please leave a review. Your reviews inspire us to continue writing about the world of spooky and untold horrors!

Check out these best-selling books from our talented authors

Ron Ripley (Ghost Stories)
- Berkley Street Series Books 1 – 9
  www.scarestreet.com/berkleyfullseries
- Moving in Series Box Set Books 1 – 6
  www.scarestreet.com/movinginboxfull

A. I. Nasser (Supernatural Suspense)
- Slaughter Series Books 1 – 3 Bonus Edition
  www.scarestreet.com/slaughterseries

David Longhorn (Sci-Fi Horror)
- Nightmare Series: Books 1 – 3
  www.scarestreet.com/nightmarebox
- Nightmare Series: Books 4 – 6
  www.scarestreet.com/nightmare4-6

Sara Clancy (Supernatural Suspense)
- Banshee Series Books 1 – 6
  www.scarestreet.com/banshee1-6

For a complete list of our new releases and best-selling horror books, visit www.scarestreet.com/books

See you in the shadows,
Team Scare Street

Made in the USA
Las Vegas, NV
31 January 2021